# When the Dead Walk in West Virginia

## Scary Stories and Creepy Folk Tales to Keep You Up at Night

Jannette Quackenbush

ISBN-13: 978-1-940087-72-6

Jannette Quackenbush

# Where's My Big Toe?

### There was an Old Woman Who Lived in a Cabin

They say old Marnie Cottrill lived alone in a collapsing cabin tucked up a holler so steep the crows had to fly sideways to get to it. She was known for brewing cough syrups, treating spider bites, and talking to things that weren't there. One spring, while digging in her garden for bloodroot and dandelion, she struck something not quite stone and not quite wood.

### She Dug Something Up

It was a toe. A big one.

Greyed like a mushroom, thick and bloated.

She pulled it free, brushed off the dirt, and found it still had a ragged edge of flesh where it had been torn, not cut.

**She Boiled It Up**

Marnie, never wasteful, boiled it in onion broth.

Ate it with cornbread and greens.

That night, the wind howled through the chimney like someone crying underwater.

**And It Came for the Toe**

Marnie sat in her rocker, sipping sassafras tea, when she heard it—

"Wherrre...

Wherrre's...

myyy biggg tooooe?"

The sound came from outside.

Near the woodpile.

She stoked the fire and locked the door.

But later—closer now—

"Wherrre...

Wherrre's...

myyy biggg tooooe?"

The voice scratched along the porch like a broom dragged slow. Then—

*Creeeak.*

The door.

It opened on its own.

Marnie reached for her old shotgun, but her hands wouldn't move.

Couldn't move.

Froze to her lap like the cold had crawled inside her veins.

A shadow entered.

Tall. Sagging. Split-footed.

And wet.

Its face was a blur of rot, with eyes that dripped like thawing candles.

"Youuuu...

...got my toe..."

The next morning, the preacher came up to check on her.

Found the cabin empty.

But on the hearth?

A pot of toe broth, still steaming.

And next to it?

A second toe.

# Bloody Bones "To eat you up with..."

### There Once was a Little Girl

In the hills near the creeks that run red with rust and old memories, where trees grow close enough to whisper, there was once a little girl who was left alone too often.

Her parents had to work the night shift at a mill far down the valley, and they would lock the cabin door behind them and say,

"Don't talk to nobody. Don't let nobody in."

And then they were gone.

**She was Lonely**

The girl would sit quietly, rocking on the porch or by the hearth. But the nights got long, and the silence got heavy, and on one such night, when the wind pushed against the cabin walls like a hand trying to get in, the girl stood by the stairwell and said:

"I wish someone would come play with me."

And from somewhere beneath the floorboards, or the dark under the stairs, came a voice.

"I'm coming soon."

She blinked.

The fire crackled.

The shadows didn't move, but something in them listened.

Later, she asked again—lonely, small: "Won't someone come play with me?"

And the voice came again.

"I'm almost there..."

The girl went back to rocking, uneasy now but still curious.

The wind outside grew still.

The cabin breathed.

She asked a third time.

And that's when she heard it—

*Thump.*

*Thump.*

*thumpety-thumpety-thump-thump.*

Something was coming down the stairs.

A head.

Raw and red.

No skin.

Just gristle and teeth like yellow fence pickets.

**Rawhead**.

Bloody Bones.

It rolled to her feet and then grew tall—too tall, stretching up into the dark above the lantern glow. It grinned down at her.

"Who are you?" she whispered.

"Bloody Bones," it smiled. "Rawhead," it grinned.

"I came to play."

She tried to be brave the way children do.

"What long fingernails you have," she said.

"To scratch you with."

"What big red eyes you have."

"To see you in the dark."

"And what big teeth you have."

"To eat you up with."

The wind returned, gusty and wild, howling against the cabin.

When her parents came home, the door was still locked.

The fire was still burning.

The chair still rocked.

And at the foot of the stairs was nothing but a small pile of bloody bones.

They buried what was left by the creek, and no one speaks her name anymore.

But sometimes, if you're out past dark in the hollers, and you say out loud that you're lonely...you might hear the voice answer back:

"I'm coming soon."

"I'm almost there..."

*Thump.*

*Thump.*

*thumpety-thumpety-thump-thump.*

# Flat Man of Vinegar Hill

In the earliest days of Benton's Ferry, the town was simple—gravel streets, sagging porches, smoke curling from stovepipes like whispers. A few families, a ferry across the Tygart River, and just enough law to make folks behave during daylight. The river was the lifeblood then. First, there were canoes, then rowboats, and finally, hulking paddlewheel steamboats that churned water thick as molasses and left behind more than just wake trails. Alongside the docks, taverns, boarding houses, and sin bloomed like fungus.

And at the top of a winding ridge beyond the river, three brothers kept a secret in barrels.

They lived up on Vinegar Hill in a squat log cabin surrounded by scrub pine and blackberry bramble. Locals thought they made cider or maybe homemade pickles. But those barrels? The ones they rolled down to town and marked "VINEGAR," those were full of moonshine strong enough to kill a bishop.

## The Barrel That Took a Man Flat

One stormy night, the brothers got into their own supply. Thunder shook the roof, and the wind howled through the gaps in the logs like something trying to get in with teeth. But the booze was flowing, and they had a wagonload of "vinegar" ready for the inns below.

The mule didn't like the storm, but it walked the hill with that tired, stubborn patience only old animals know. The wagon groaned behind it, barrels clinking with every jolt in the muddy road.

Then lightning cracked like God's whip overhead— and the mule stopped cold.

A barrel up top shifted.

Wobbled.

Tipped.

It rolled with purpose, like it had picked its target, and struck the youngest brother square in the chest, knocking him flat to the ground.

The other two sat stunned, slack-jawed in the rain. They heard him cry out just once. Then again—a raspier sound, as if the wind were caught in his lungs.

But when they climbed down and tried to shove the barrel off...

...it wouldn't budge.

They finally rolled it off. But what was left underneath wasn't a man anymore.

It was something like a rag flattened by hooves, skin bloated from the pressure, face purple and wide, tongue split. His bones had been mashed into the mud like old straw.

They buried him on top of Vinegar Hill in the family plot.

They poured liquor on his grave and tried not to speak his name.

But the hill never forgot.

**The Thing That Rises**

On stormy nights—when the thunder rolls across the ridge like a wagon with no brakes, and lightning turns the mist the color of old bruises—people driving Vinegar Hill Road see something.

First, it's two glowing spots, side by side in the fog, low to the ground—like eyes where no creature crouches.

Then comes the fog. It wraps the eyes in mist, rising like steam from a boiling grave. And when it pulls back, there's something standing there:

A man. But not quite.

He's flat. Too flat.

His chest curves inward, his limbs are too thin, and he moves like a kite caught in low wind. Waving. Wobbling.

Beckoning.

He stumbles forward with that same old clap—slapping his palms together in rhythm like he's keeping time to a song only the dead can hear.

Then he stops. Tilts his head. And screams—high and reedy, like air blowing through a split in wet wood.

He vanishes just before the graveyard at the top of the hill.

And if you followed him?

You might find your tires flattened.

Your skin is bruised without cause.

Or worse, you'll hear something roll toward you in the dark.

And you'll know it's your turn.

They say he dances now every time the thunder walks.

Because some spirits don't rise.

They stagger.

They roll.

And they flatten everything in their way.

# Tailypo

### A Woodsman Lived in a Cabin

Long ago, deep in a tangle of woods where even the trees seemed to whisper, there lived an old woodsman in a cabin stitched together with moss and mud. The place sagged under age and rot. In winter, the wind slipped through every crack like a knife, and the only company the man had were his three hounds—I Know, You Know, and Calico.

One night, starving and shaking from cold, something wriggled through the wall—a thing like a rat, but longer.

### He Sliced off the Tail and Ate it

A sinewy beast with a tail that curled like a question mark. The old man swung his hatchet, sharp from use, and sliced the tail clean off. The thing screamed and vanished.

The man tossed the tail in the fire, roasted it to a crisp, and ate it.

### Then the Thing Came for its Tail

That night, he slept full for the first time in weeks.

But then came the scratching.

And the voice.

"Tailypo... Tailypo... all I want is my Tailypo..."

He bolted upright. "I don't have your Tailypo tail! Get gone, and don't come back!"

The scratching stopped.

Then, it started again—closer.

The man threw open the door. "Hey, hey!" he shouted. His dogs took off into the trees, growling into the dark.

Minutes passed. Then a yelp.

### Only You Know and Calico returned.

Again, the scratching. Again, the voice, now angrier:

"Tailypo... Tailypo... all I want is my Tailypo..."

"Go away!" the man screamed.

Again, the dogs gave chase.

Another yelp.

### Only Calico came back.

When the scratching returned, it came from inside the walls. From the roof. From the floorboards.

The voice came, growling now:

"Tailypo... Tailypo... all I want is my Tailypo..."

He sent Calico out.

Another yelp.

Then silence.

The final scratching came just before dawn. The voice, snarling from behind the door:

"Tailypo... Tailypo... all I want is my Tailypo..."

The man grabbed his hatchet. "I told you—I don't have it!" he shouted.

From the dark came the answer:

"Oh yes, you do..."

He stepped out, hatchet raised.

And then the woods swallowed him whole.

Some say the thing got its tail back.

Some say it took more.

The cabin is long gone, only a chimney left standing like a tooth from the earth. But on moonlit nights, when wind cuts through the trees like claws, you might hear it—scratching.

And a voice, calling:

"Tailypo... Tailypo..."

Before it fades into the dark.

# The Cross-Tie Crone of Dunlow

### When the Rails Were King

In the early days, when iron rails stitched through the hills like veins through a corpse, Dunlow thrashed with life. They called it Twelvepole at first, back when the Norfolk & Western Railroad tore through the woods in 1892, bringing a flood of settlers and the reek of coal smoke. A town rose fast—a crooked schoolhouse, a sagging church, a hotel where whiskey sloshed and fists flew. By winter, nearly two hundred souls scratched out a living under the railroad's black breath.

Then came December 1901.

A fire, wild as a rabid dog, ripped through the town. Wooden beams popped like gunshots, and glass wept itself to dust. What wasn't burned was left blackened and hollow. After the fire, the mines shriveled. The trains slowed. By 1933, the tracks lay half-dead, like the bones of a thing no one dared bury.

But not everything that clung to the rails was willing to die.

### The Witch of the Tracks

Old trainmen muttered about her over their whiskey glasses — a hunched, barefoot crone who stalked the railbeds at the lip of dusk, dragging burlap sacks that writhed and twitched.

They said the bags were stuffed with dead crows, bloated toads, teeth, and things too mangled to name. Anything she poke-poke-poked with a gnarled stick that did not move fast enough to escape, she plucked up between knobby-knuckled finger and thumb. While it writhed and squirmed in her fist, she stuffed it into her bag.

Her dress sagged in tatters, stitched and pinned with rusted nails, each one driven through rags steeped in graveyard mud.

You could smell her before you saw her — a reek of sulfur, old blood, and wet ashes curling on the wind.

She laid curses on the cross-ties — things knotted in twine, things that pulsed and bled if you looked too close.

If a man was fool enough to step on a rail tie that stank of brimstone, it was said he'd carry her mark in his bones.

One engineer — a young fellow, full of spit and pride — swore he saw her face leering out of the locomotive's firebox, all scorched grin and bleeding gums.

He died screaming before he could wrench the brakes, his last breath a howl that shattered every window in the station house.

His body was pulled from the wreckage, half-cooked, mouth open so wide it looked like his jaw had been broken trying to spit out her name.

### If You Must Walk the Rails

If you ever find yourself on the tracks at sunset, and the woods grow too quiet, and the mist hangs low like a shroud — watch your step.

If you catch the smell of sulfur, sharp and choking, it's already too late.

Step wrong, and she'll crawl into your dreams with her sack of twitching dead things.

She'll press her nails into your chest while you sleep.

She'll whisper in your ear until the sheets go damp with sweat.

And night after night, you'll wake burning, burning, burning, until there's nothing left but smoke curling up from your own blackened bones.

# Hedger Hollow: The Living Don't Linger There After Dark

### The Waters Should be Feared

It moves like something alive.

The Little Kanawha River, winding and writhing through Braxton, Gilmer, and Calhoun Counties, doesn't rush—it coils. A black ribbon cut through stone and time, carrying oil, lumber, and settlers who once believed they could tame what could not be tamed. The Shawnee called it Keninsheka—the River of Evil Spirits. And they were right to fear it.

Its currents tug from beneath, unseen, forming whirlpools that grasp like fingers with no flesh. They do not pull you down to drown.

They hold you.

And they do not let go.

## Coins and Cold Dead Hands

Not all who died in that river were taken by nature.

There were men who stalked its edges, hiding behind dogwoods and drifts of mist—murderers, drawn not by vengeance but by greed. They watched the peddlers who moved between Parkersburg, Burning Springs, and Creston. Men carrying bolts of cloth, medicine tins, small jugs of oil—and worse, money.

One such man was Hedger.

He was a familiar sight, trundling his wagon along the river road, his voice like gravel, his wares honest and humble. One day, he never made it to Industry.

Some say he was followed. Others say he trusted the wrong face in a tavern or home. Either way, his body was found days later, drifting just beneath the surface at a place the locals still call Devil's Run—a snag of rotted logs knotted like a trap. His throat had been slit, his pockets turned out. And his eyes… were still open.

## Hedger's Country

They dragged his corpse to the shore in silence. Laid him on the rocks near a bend in the river so sharp it looked like the land recoiled. He was buried not far from the Belt Cemetery, up near Low Gap. No headstone.

Just earth and rot.

But the river does not forget.

That stretch of water—four miles between Industry and Creston—became known as Hedger's Country. And even now, the living don't linger there after dark.

### The Stranger on the River Path

One evening, as fog hung low over the shallows, a young man and his uncle walked the narrow footpath along the river's edge. The trail twisted between a black locust tree and a sunken patch of mud. As they stepped aside to let a stranger pass, they waited. And waited.

No footsteps. No voice. No breath.

When they turned back, the figure was gone.

The uncle spat on the ground. "Shouldn't have come here after sundown."

### Screams from the Water

Others have heard the ghost. Shrieks rising from the riverbed, like a man being gutted again and again. If you call back, shout into the dark—Hedger! Hedger! Hedger!

It gets louder.

Closer.

### Call it Again. See What Happens

They say if you go to Devil's Run when the moon is high and call out his name three times, the water begins to churn. Not wildly—purposefully. Like something moving toward you, dragging chains beneath the surface. If you wait, if you don't run, you'll hear it— splashes, closer and closer—until whatever's coming reaches the bank.

No one knows what happens if you let it reach you.

But once, a traveler who dared the ritual was found the next morning on the opposite bank, lying stiff and soaked in riverweed. His face was pale. His lips were blue.

He never spoke again.

**Last Warning—Never Say Hedger Three Times**

There are places where the land forgets its dead.

This is not one of them.

The Little Kanawha remembers—every scream, every stolen breath.

It does not forgive. It does not sleep.

And if you dare to call Hedger's name, do not expect silence.

If you linger too long—if your feet freeze and your courage fails—the splashing will come.

Closer.

Hungrier.

And by the time the sun cracks open the sky, you'll be on the other side of the river.

And you won't be alone…because, as the old saying goes, *if "Hedger, Hedger, Hedger," you cry. When you wake up in the morning, you'll be on the other side.*

# Silver Run Tunnel: White Woman of Silver Run

### The Tracks Still Cry Out

The Baltimore & Ohio line once ran like a vein through the hills of West Virginia, dragging freight and midnight steamers through coal towns, past lonely switch houses, and into the black throat of Tunnel #19, just outside of Cairo. They called it Silver Run.

But the tracks don't sing anymore.

They've been torn up.

The shriek of steel has quieted.

And now, all that's left are bones in the dark and something still walking.

**First Sight**

He was young then—an engineer hauling the midnight express out of Grafton, headed west to Parkersburg. Thirty miles in, just past the shadow of Smithburg Tunnel, the train was rolling steady when the fog thickened.

There, in the moonlight and the weak glow of the engine, she stood—a woman in white, walking the rails like she was sleepwalking through a graveyard. Her hair was black and matted down her back. Her gown trailed the ground. And on her feet were gold slippers, tarnished now, dulled with dirt and time.

He panicked.

Threw the brakes.

But the train couldn't stop fast enough.

And the woman... glided lazily forward. Not walking. Floating inches above the track, turning her head too slowly, like something with a broken neck.

When they halted the train, she was gone—swallowed whole by fog so thick it stung the eyes. The engineer, the conductor, the fireman—they searched.

They called out.

But the rails rang hollow.

They left with sweat freezing on their backs.

**She Came Again**

The next night, the engineer was on his usual run.

He told himself it was a trick of the light. A story to keep yardmen nervous and half-drunk. But she was there again—clearer this time, the moon catching the pin of a jeweled brooch gleaming at her pale collarbone.

He stopped the train. He watched.

She vanished with a low, animal moan that didn't fade—it cut off like something had snapped her throat shut.

Men began whispering.

They stopped walking the tracks alone.

They locked doors in the depots, even in daylight.

## O'Flannery's Run

Then came O'Flannery, loud-mouthed and mean.

"Ghosts?" he spat. "I'll run the bitch through."

One fog-choked night, she waited.

She stood in the middle of the track, her pale dress rippling without wind. Her arms didn't move. Her head was tilted like she'd been listening for something in the rails.

O'Flannery didn't slow down.

He blew through her.

He laughed about it. Until he got to Parkersburg.

## She Rode the Cowcatcher

The telegraphs were already humming.

Every signalman, every switch tender, every half-asleep section man from Cairo to Slate—they all saw her.

Clinging to the cowcatcher of O'Flannery's engine— her dead eyes wide, her dress soaked, her jaw hanging slack as if she'd been screaming the whole way.

O'Flannery couldn't stop shaking when he stepped off the train.

## What They Dug Up

Years passed. The young engineer grew old.

And then came the news—a skeleton was unearthed by workmen clearing a cellar foundation near the ruins of a house along the old line.

The bones were dried with flakes of skin still clinging.

Her ribs were broken. Her skull cracked in three places.

One slipper was still gold. The other was missing.

And clutched in one bony hand—a brooch.

Jeweled. Still glinting.

No grave marker. Just stones and rot and the rusted shadow of the tracks above.

## Silver Run Doesn't Sleep

The B&O line was shut down in 1985. The tracks were pulled. The whistles fell silent. But some things don't leave. At night, hikers on the North Bend Rail Trail claim to hear a sound that doesn't belong in a forest—the distant wail of a whistle rolling low across the trees.

And sometimes—a moan follows it. If you're near Tunnel #19, you might see something pale move between the trees. You might catch the glint of a slipper or the shimmer of old bone in the fog.

And if the rails had voices, they'd tell you this:

She didn't vanish. She was buried alive in stone and screams. And now, she walks the old line.

Still waiting for the train that never stopped.

# Ritchie Mines: A Million Dollars and a Mountain Full of Bones

### The Ground Remembers

In the mountains of West Virginia, where the trees come together so tightly you can barely see the sky is a town nearly forgotten—choked by vines, buried beneath dead leaves, and mostly disregarded.

Ritchie Mines, they called it. But the locals whisper it's something else now.

Something hungrier.

## A Million Dollars and a Mountain of Bones

It began in 1852 when Frederick Lemon found something black and thick seeping from the hillside. Asphalt. Within a year, the wilderness was cleared and paved over in the name of progress. A million-dollar profit came quickly—straight into the pockets of men who never lifted a shovel. They built a towering brick hotel to survey their empire, and a full village bloomed around it: shops, schools, churches, boarding houses, and a sawmill.

But beneath it all, the earth groaned.

Crews worked from the top of the hills, carving deep into the hillside and toward the creek. They were lowered on ropes like bait into open water filled with sharks. The mine sank deeper and deeper—nearly 300 feet below Macfarlan Creek, where asphalt waited to be taken.

The deeper they went, the worse it got.

The water seeped in.

The gas grew thicker.

And the fear—that the mine itself was alive—settled into their throats like soot.

## The Watchman's Fire

One black night, the mine was left with only a watchman.

He never came out.

A gas explosion ripped through the pit like a hell-born scream, and when the sun rose, all that remained was a scorched hole in the mountain.

The body was never recovered.

Even the stone had cracked and blackened.

They say he didn't scream. He just opened his mouth, and the flame took his voice first.

## A Year of Ash

In 1873, another grisly tragedy struck—three men vaporized in another explosion. Their remains were smeared against the shaft walls like charcoal fingerprints.

But it was the following year, 1874, that the mine claimed its darkest tithe.

A larger detonation collapsed a horizontal tunnel, entombing thirty miners alive. Their cries echoed from beneath the rubble for hours. Maybe longer. But the walls had shifted, and the mine had decided to keep them.

Some say they died clawing at the ceiling.

Others claim they were swallowed into the asphalt at the bottom of the shaft—screaming as it filled their lungs with black.

Their bodies were never recovered.

And the men above stopped digging.

They stopped speaking, too.

## The Curse That Festered

Soon, no one would step into the shaft after dark.

Not even with pay in hand.

Workers whispered of shadows that moved where no light could reach. Some claimed to see figures down the old shaft—faces half-burned, eyes like coal-white stones, watching from the cracks in the wall.

Tools were found bent in ways that made no sense.

Boot prints appeared where no man had walked.

And when they tried to revive the operation, machines refused to run.

It was said that the mine had gone mad. Or perhaps the land had grown tired of feeding the rich.

## A Town That Sank Into Silence

By the time the coal vein was lost in 1874, the community had begun to rot.

The schoolhouse windows were shattered by the wind. The grand brick hotel stood silent as a tomb.

The village crumbled. Families drifted to Silver Run and Oxbow, leaving behind only the stories.

Of moaning at dusk.

Of lantern lights flickering in tunnels that had been sealed for years.

Of ghostly miners, their mouths stuffed with ash, still crawling toward the surface.

A few stayed.

They never spoke of what they saw—only that something still moved in the shaft after sundown.

## They Never Reached the Top

They say several miners were buried alive, their lungs filling not with smoke but silence.

And those souls?

They didn't die peacefully. The immigrant workers believed those who remained behind were cursed to roam the mines, searching for the men who left them there. Their bones twisted by flame, their eyes burned out, their spirits oozing from the cracks like black pitch.

They aren't lost.

They're waiting.

## The Shaft Still Breathes

Today, Ritchie Mines lies in ruins, hidden in thickets of thorns and heavy oak, its carved stone boulevard now crumbling under moss and shadow. A creek runs through it.

But the mine?

It still breathes.

Each gust from its ruined mouth is a whisper from below—not wind, but warning.

And if you find it—if you feel the unnatural chill rising from its throat, do not speak.

Do not peer into its depths.

Because something down there is awake.

And watching.

It remembers the boots that stood safe at the surface while others choked and burned in the dark.

It remembers the laughter of men who cashed checks as others were buried alive beneath stone and ash.

And if it mistakes you for one of them…it won't let you leave.

Not whole.

Not alive.

Only burning,

only screaming,

only another echo in the black.

# Burnt House: The Girl Who Danced in Fire

### The Road That Forgot Itself

Drive along State Route 47—the old Stanton-Parkersburg Turnpike—through Ritchie County, and you might think little of it.

A narrow road, choked by trees and twisting through small towns, most of which aren't on any map and have names long forgotten.

But once, in the mid-1800s, it was a lifeline.

A road carved into the bones of the mountains — the only thread between the Shenandoah Valley and the bustling Ohio River in Parkersburg.

Coaches rattled over it thrice a week, their wheels chewing through dirt and stone, carrying letters, traders, and the already-doomed across nine counties.

Inns sprouted like weeds along the way — thrown up wherever the dark seemed a little less eager, wherever the woods didn't seem quite so hungry.

One such stop was called Grass Run.

And Grass Run had a secret the earth still remembers.

**The Inn That Should Never Have Stood**

In 1836, John Harris, with his son William and three enslaved souls, raised a three-story stagecoach inn—a crooked, leaning thing of rotting wood and low ceilings, its windows staring blankly over a creek that never ran clean.

It prospered for a time.

The mail was delivered.

Peddlers came, heavy with wares.

The tavern choked with the stench of sweat and spilled drink, the halls shivering with laughter that curdled the longer you listened.

But the townsfolk watched.

And whispered.

They noticed one enslaved girl in particular — Delores.

Young. Delicate. Dressed too fine—lace and jewelry that should have still been packed away in a peddler's cart, not hung from her slender neck.

No one dared speak it outright.

But they saw the signs.

And they remembered the faces of the peddlers who arrived...and were never seen again.

Rumor told of a boy in the stables who saw William Harris slit a pack peddler's throat ear-to-ear—the blood falling in a river onto the dirt.

The body dragged across the turnpike to a hollow that would come to bear its name: Dead Man's Hollow.

Locals said they saw Delores scrubbing the wooden floors raw — the stains stubborn, black, too much like ground bone and clotting blood.

**The Fire in Her Eyes**

By the 1850s, the tavern's good fortune rotted.

Rumors fermented under the floorboards like corpses rot in fresh graves in deep summer.

Travelers whispered of screams splitting the night.

Of doors that opened onto rooms that didn't exist.

Of glimpses of Delores, barefoot in the yard, her face twisted, her eyes alight with something hotter than hatred.

Sometimes, they heard howls drifting up from Dead Man's Hollow—low, broken things that sounded half-human.

Harris sold the inn.

Sold the girl.

The Groves family took possession — of both the house and her.

And that's when the story cracked open like a rib.

## She Danced While It Burned

The Groves prepared to send Delores back to her former owner.

Instead, she set fire to a heap of clothes upstairs.

Or so they said.

Some called it revenge.

Some called it madness.

But those who stood outside, helpless in the thick night air, saw more.

They saw her—through the warped glass of the lookout window—spinning barefoot in the blaze, her arms wide.

Her silhouette rippled in the smoke, twisting and writhing as the fire chewed through the beams.

They said her mouth hung open in laughter—a sound swallowed by the roar of flame.

And even as the roof split and fell, she did not stop.

She danced as the building caved in around her.

She danced even as the flames licked her skin black and split.

## The House That Would Not Die

For years, the skeleton of the tavern lingered—a blackened husk sagging beside the road reeking of old burned wood and a grisly marker of things undead.

Drivers would not stop.

Locals crossed themselves as they passed.

The name stuck: *Burnt House*.

But the fire was never truly put out.

## Ashes in the Air

On nights when the fog clots thick in the hollows, passersby say they see it — a flicker, a shimmer, a shape.

First, the smoke.

Then, the outline.

Then the full, shuddering figure of a girl — wreathed in ash, her hair alight like candle wicks, her skin blistered gray.

She dances still—over nothing but memory and cinders—her mouth split wide in a smile that has no end.

Those who swear they hear it claim the air hums when she appears—the low, awful groan of old wood about to break.

## They Built Over Her Bones

Someone, foolish or blind, built a house atop the scorched ruin.

They say the walls breathe in winter.

They say soot drifts down the chimneys even when there is no fire.

They say the parlor reeks of burnt cloth and blistered flesh. Because she never left.

Because the earth itself remembers.

And if you pass along Route 47 and catch a glimpse of something burning deep in the trees — do not stop.

Do not look too long. Because if you do, she may turn— Smile through blackened, broken teeth—And offer you her hand.

And once you take it, she will never let you go.

Because she still wants to dance out her revenge.

# The Lantern Keeper of Coopers Rock

Long ago, a story drifted like smoke from one ridge to the next—passed between tired miners over black coffee, murmured by firelight, and eventually scratched into the pages of the West Virginia Folklore Collection: "There is an old man who walks with a lantern down the forest edge, always in fog, always when the moon is out. They say he was a deserter who lit fires to guide others out, but no one ever made it home." —WVARHC, early 1900s

But that was just the beginning.

### The Barrel-Maker's Refuge

Coopers Rock State Forest, perched atop Cheat Mountain, seems peaceful now. Trails wind through forests thick with laurel. Lookouts give way to dizzying drops over Cheat River Gorge. But beneath your boots are stories. And under those? Bones.

During the Civil War, the forest became a refuge—not for soldiers, but for those who ran from war.

Among them was Elijah Boring, a Union deserter from Grafton.

Some said he was a coward.

Others swore he refused an execution order and fled, carrying only his lantern, a knife, and the weight of what he'd seen.

He became a kind of outlaw—a cooper by trade who stole lumber and built barrels to barter with mountain folk. He dug himself a home near an old logging camp and lived like a ghost among the living, scavenging onions and raiding wagons for bread. As others found their way to him—Confederate, Union, lost boys with bleeding feet—he lit fires in the hills to guide them in.

He wasn't a hero.

But he was something like a shepherd of the damned.

### A Storm. A Light. Then Nothing.

In 1864, under a lightning-cracked sky, Elijah went out to meet a young runaway—another deserter, lost in the gorge. Witnesses claimed to see a lantern swinging in the storm, bobbing unnaturally near a narrow crag where the rocks were known to slip.

The light danced wildly.

Then blinked out.

In the morning, they found torn cloth, drag marks, and the scent of kerosene—but no Elijah. No runaway. Only a trail of footprints stopped at the edge of the gorge.

### The Light Still Walks

Time passed, but Elijah didn't stay buried.

The stories say he still walks the forest—his lantern glowing ten feet off the ground, his coat never wet, even in a downpour. The flame never flickers. The light never wavers. And those who follow it?

They don't always return.

In 1967, two hikers chased the lantern down a trail near Rock City, a crevasse between towering rock formations. They were found the next day, disoriented and shivering. "We could see our breath," one said, "in the middle of June."

In 2002, a camper followed the light off-trail. He came back shaken and scratched to pieces. "It led me to an old mine entrance," he whispered. "But that mine ain't on any map."

In 2015, a photographer captured a soft orb of light hovering midair—right where no trail leads. Local legend says: If the lantern turns to face you, you'll never find your way back.

### But He's Not Alone

Some say the forest has two keepers now.

In the 1930s, a coal miner was sent to check for gas in a narrow shaft just off the ridge. He did not return.

When they went in after him, they only found his lantern still burning in the soot.

The tunnel was black and slick with melted stone.

There was no body.

But some say he burned alive when the gas ignited—lungs seared shut, eyes boiled, mouth open in a scream that no one heard.

His spirit, they say, never left.

He walks not with a light to guide but to warn. And sometimes, at night, in the deeper woods, you'll see not one but two lanterns. One gliding smooth and silent. The other—jerking.

Twitching.

Flickering like the breath of something dying.

**A Final Warning**

If you see the light at Coopers Rock—don't follow.

Don't call out.

And for God's sake, don't ask for directions.

Because one of them wants to lead you home.

And the other wants to watch you burn.

# The Hollowed Halls of the Trans-Allegheny Lunatic Asylum

**The Hollowed Halls of the Trans-Allegheny Lunatic Asylum...and One Moan Heard Too Close to the Stomach**

There's something wrong with the bones of that building. You can feel it the second you step through the doors of the Trans-Allegheny Lunatic Asylum—the way the air settles wrong in your lungs. The way the echo of your footsteps seems to walk ahead of you, as if something already knows you're there.

It was once called the Weston State Hospital, and though it closed in 1994, parts of it still seem alive. Or at least undead.

They broke ground in 1858, but the war interrupted—Union soldiers camped there, smoked their cigarettes between unfinished walls, and left more than just muddy footprints in the mortar. It opened in 1864, meant to hold 250 souls, but it swelled and festered until over 2,400 lived and died inside its stone ribs. It was shut down after lawsuits, neglect, starvation, and whispers of things you don't talk about at dinner.

Now, it stands preserved for history. And for ghosts.

I know—I've been there.

## A Moan in the Wrong Key

I brought my two kids along once. One was 14, the other 9. I'd skipped supper to make the final tour of the day—because, of course, the best ghosts come out just before the lights go out.

The guide had us sit in the long, decaying hallway outside a room where moaning is often heard—long-dead voices still echoing from their padded prisons.

It was deathly quiet.

Then it began.

A low moan.

Soft at first.

Then climbing, groaning, rising into a wail so guttural and wrong that a woman near the wall leapt to her feet. People gasped. One woman covered her ears.

Another started to cry.

It was the sound of a soul trying to claw its way back through stone.

Except...

It was my stomach roaring greedily.

Hollow. Ravenous. Demonic.

Growling loud enough to resurrect the staff.

My kids stared at me in silent horror, teeth clenched, eyes wide, knowing precisely what I'd done—but never betraying me. Meanwhile, the group fled the hall, led by a guide who assumed a ghost had just awakened.

We never spoke of it again.

**But That's Where the Laughing Stops**

Because some stories from the asylum are far less funny.

### • The Screamer in Ward F

This was where they kept the worst of them—the violent ones. Men who beat others bloody and screamed at walls long after their minds had emptied.

One such man screamed for days. No one stopped him. They assumed it was just more madness.

Then they found him.

Dead.

He'd bitten off part of his own tongue, and the walls were slick with something like spit and blood.

Now, you still hear him—deep, rattling howls that vibrate the floorboards. Tour groups report the cold before they hear it. Some catch a whisper on recording devices: not words, just the sound of a man who never learned how to die quietly.

### • Ruth's Room

Ruth was committed in the 1950s for violent outbursts. She bit, scratched, howled. They tried to sedate her. They tried isolation.

She died with her hands still curled into claws.

Now, her wheelchair moves on its own. Visitors report being pushed. Scratched. One guide claims he saw the indentation of a body in the chair when the room was empty.

The window she used to scream through?

Sometimes, it fogs up from the inside, and you can see a face pressed to it.

### • The Suicide Bathroom

No plumbing. No running water.

But they say you still hear dripping.

And the mirror—cracked and stained—has shown figures standing behind guests.

One woman swore she saw her own reflection turn toward her, smile, and step closer.

She fainted before she could run.

### • The Children's Ward

Children were kept here—those misdiagnosed, epileptic, or just inconvenient.

At night, the toys move.

Visitors hear skipping, giggling, and the unmistakable roll of a ball on a wooden floor.

But on full moons, the laughter changes.

It becomes a whisper: "Don't tell." And no one does.

### • The Locked Room in the Attic

For years, it was hidden. No one went in. They rediscovered it during renovations.

It smelled like mildew and old sweat. It had scratch marks on the wall. And on the plaster, barely legible in the dark, were words: LET ME OUT

Some say they vanish when the lights are on.

But they're there when it's dark.

Always.

There are places in this world that don't forget.

They hold sound like a jar holds smoke. They preserve fear like pickled meat. And the Trans-Allegheny Lunatic Asylum?

It doesn't just remember.

It repeats.

# Staunton-Parkersburg Turnpike: Phantom Hitchhiker

**The Staunton-Parkersburg Turnpike**

The Staunton-Parkersburg Turnpike is older than it looks.

Winding like a scar across the Appalachian spine, it was carved into the hills with blood and blasted stone. Meant to connect Staunton, Virginia, to Parkersburg, West Virginia, the road was the 19th century's answer to traveling through the wilderness.

Claudius Crozet, an engineer with grand visions and a reputation for stubbornness, led its construction in 1831. But the land fought back—swallowing money, mules, and men with equal hunger. It wasn't finished until 1847, and even then, some claimed the mountain had never entirely given it up.

During the Civil War, it became a lifeline and a graveyard. Armies clawed their way along its hairpin curves. Supply wagons overturned. Men were ambushed, bled out into the dirt, or dragged screaming into the trees by the half-mad and the starving. More than a few soldiers vanished on that road without a trace, their final cries muffled by wind and musket smoke.

After the war, the turnpike faded into a quieter life.

The trains came. Time moved on.

But the road?

The road stayed hungry.

### The Hitchhiker Who Isn't There

It was sometime in the early '90s when a man named Tim Miller was driving a stretch of the old turnpike ahead of a summer storm. A winding curve, thick with trees. The kind of place where the sun only hits the ground in shards.

That's when he saw a man walking the shoulder, perfectly upright in the gloom. He was wearing white bellbottoms, a clean T-shirt, and no jacket—odd, given the chill rising in the wind.

Tim slowed. In his words, "I used to hitchhike all over the country in the seventies. Didn't think twice about picking somebody up."

The stranger got in without a word. Closed the door gently. No nod. No greeting. Just sat there.

And that's when Tim smelled it.

Not sweat. Not cigarettes. Something wet and rotting, like river mud and decay, or meat forgotten in a cooler under the July sun. The smell assaulted his nose like a two-day dead skunk on a hot asphalt road in mid-August.

Then the hitchhiker spoke. Just three words:

"Jesus is coming."

Tim turned his head. The seat was empty.

**And He Keeps Coming Back**

Tim's wasn't the only story. Not even close.

Dozens of travelers over the decades—truckers, nurses, off-duty cops—have all described the same man. Neatly dressed. Silent. A faint, unnatural odor.

And the same thing happens:

He gets in.

He says, "Jesus is coming."

Then he's gone.

The doors stay locked. The seatbelt is still clicked. In some cases, he leaves behind wet footprints on the floormat. Others say they feel him breathing just behind their right ear for a moment after he vanishes.

One state trooper reported picking him up on a foggy night in Wirt County. Said the man was already in the backseat by the time he noticed—no memory of stopping. He turned around to speak... and found an empty pair of handcuffs lying on the seat. He never filed a report. Said he'd lose his badge if he did.

## The Road Remembers

The old-timers say the man was a soldier from the war—a deserter who shot his captain and was caught along the turnpike during a thunderstorm. They chained him up in the back of a wagon to haul him to Parkersburg for hanging. But somewhere near Burnt House, the whole party disappeared.

Just the wagon remained.

The chains were snapped.

The ground was torn up like something had dragged itself free.

Others believe he's something else entirely.

Not a ghost.

Not a man.

Just a warning.

Because "Jesus is coming" may not be a prophecy.

It may be a confession.

So, if you drive that road... and see a man in white walking the shoulder in the storm—keep going.

Don't slow down.

Don't look in the mirror.

And whatever you do...

Don't let him in.

# The Screaming Thing of Paddle Creek

Deep in the tangle of West Virginia's forested heart, where hollers twist like broken fingers, and the wind forgets how to move, flows a narrow, dark ribbon called Paddle Creek. It's not a place people talk about much. And when they do, they speak low—because some sounds shouldn't be remembered.

Out there, past the last gravel pull-off, where the trees press in tight, and cell signals choke, something screams.

## The Sound That Cuts Through Bone

It starts as a whimper.

Something small. Something begging.

Like a child—frightened, wet, alone, but then it grows.

Higher. Sharper. More wrong. It climbs like a fire gutting the lungs until it sounds like a woman being torn open by something too large to see.

And just as your ears catch it and your spine begins to curl, it vanishes. Only to shriek again from the other side of the trees.

Instantly.

As if the thing has no body. Or too many.

Locals call it *The Screaming Thing.* They always have. Because there's never been a better name.

## A Thing Older Than Echoes

It's been there as long as the mountains. Older folks say it comes down off the ridge during storms. Younger ones say it's just wind through the gorge.

But the wind doesn't cry like a baby.

The wind doesn't laugh like a drunk woman right before the bottle smashes.

And the wind doesn't follow you home.

## The Thing They Call Whistlin' Jack

Some whisper it's a Whistlin' Jack—one of the old Appalachian monsters, half-cat, half-man, full of bad luck.

They say it walks on two legs when it pleases but runs on four when angry. It meows like a kitten, whistles like a man, and screams like something you left behind to die.

They say it lures you off the trail with voices you recognize. Sometimes, it uses your name. Sometimes, it mewls or sobs or cries like a newborn.

And when you follow it?

You don't come back.

**No Tracks. No Eyes. No Mercy.**

Many have tried to find it.

Hunters. Skeptics. Drunks with guns. None found more than empty ground, the smell of rot, and a silence so total it made their ears ache.

Whatever it is, it leaves no prints. No scat. No claw marks on the bark. Just the sense that something saw you first and let you leave.

*This time.*

**She Saw It Leap**

One story never left the mountain.

A woman—church-going, solid, plain as cornbread—was walking home at dusk when she saw a shadow move in a tree. Then another.

Then something leapt.

Black. Tall. Not human. Not beast.

It sailed over her head, silent as fog, and vanished into the hillside.

The moment it was gone, the screaming began.

Right behind her.

Right in her ear.

She ran until she felt like her lungs were bleeding. She never walked alone again.

**Stay Away From Paddle Creek**

People say the woods there are cursed.

Others say they're just leftover—left over from when the world was wild, and God hadn't finished naming the animals.

But whatever's screaming in the timber at Paddle Creek isn't trying to warn you.

It's trying to find you.

And if you hear it close—

don't follow the voice.

Don't answer back.

Don't run.

Just drop to the ground.

Cover your ears.

And pray you weren't the one it was looking for.

# The Crying Baby of Blue Jay

The town of Blue Jay bloomed like a bruise in the early 1900s—birthed by the Blue Jay Lumber Company, which stripped the hills around Big Beaver Creek of everything green and rooted. Trees fell like soldiers. Mud roads became clogged with mules, wagons, and the groan of labor that never ended.

By the mid-century, Blue Jay had faded into something quieter. Just scattered homes, a gas pump that barely worked, and the sense that something had gone wrong there long ago. No one talked about it outright.

But they crossed themselves at certain bends in the road.

And they never ever stopped in the hollow between Daniels and Blue Jay—not after dark.

## Chains That Drag with No Hands

The hospital engineer was the first to speak up, the only outsider who didn't know better. He told it plainly: "You go down that road on a moonless night, and you'll hear it. The clanking of heavy chains, like someone's still rolling logs down from the ridge. Then comes the thud, like trunks hitting packed dirt, over and over."

But no matter how many people searched with lanterns and flashlights, they never found the source.

No chains. No logs. No tracks.

Just the sound of something working in the dark, unseen but not unheard.

## The House Down the Hill

Farther along the road, where the pavement dips into a narrow gulch, and the trees knit tight like funeral lace, there used to be a house.

A man and woman lived there. No one recalls their names, only that they kept to themselves and had a baby.

And then, one day, the baby was gone.

No funeral. No fuss. Just silence—until the couple fled under cover of night, packed everything they could carry, and left no forwarding address. They didn't tell the neighbors goodbye. Didn't leave the house unlocked.

They just vanished.

And that's when the crying began.

## A Scream Not Meant for This World

At first, it sounded like a rabbit being torn apart, that high, sharp shriek that makes even the bravest flinch.

Then came the second scream—lower, rasping, as if whatever it was had lost its voice from screaming too long.

The third? It came soft.

So soft.

A baby's cry, thin and broken, ending in a moan that drifted through the branches like fog through a graveyard fence.

People stayed away after dark.

Dogs wouldn't go near the old fence posts.

And children knew better than to throw stones near the hollow because if they did—They'd hear a voice say, "Mama."

And then they would hear the sound of something crawling through the leaves toward them.

## Still Heard Today

They tore the house down long ago. Built nothing in its place. Nature tried to reclaim the land, but nothing grows quite right there.

The cries still come.

Especially when the air is thick with rain, and the trees go still, and the road glistens like a black mirror to the past.

Locals say it was never a baby at all.

That maybe the chains, the logging sounds, the screams—they're all the same thing.

That whatever happened in that house wasn't natural.

Wasn't forgivable.

And now the land remembers.

So, if you're ever driving down that road between Daniels and Blue Jay, and you hear chains dragging or a baby crying in three pitiful bursts—

Don't stop.

Don't look.

Don't speak.

And for the love of God, don't call out.

Because if you do, you might hear something call back.

And it might still be hungry—not just for a mother, but for whatever birthed it, smothered it, and left it to rot in the dark.

And this time, it doesn't want to be held.

It wants to be heard.

# The Coal Hollow Whistler

## When the Mountain Clamped Its Mouth Shut

Coal Hollow was never more than a scratch on the map — just a scatter of shanties, coal carts broken like dead legs, and blackened men stooping low under the mountain's rotten weight.

The seams were thin.

The shafts went deep.

Even the boney dump heaps were too poor to bother sifting — just black mounds of slag and crushed stone.

By the winter of 1932, the wood bracing the tunnels had turned soft as grave moss.

They say the collapse came without warning — a low, throaty groan, a sick shudder, and then the mountain clamped its mouth shut like it meant to stay shut.

Seventeen men were swallowed whole.

Not crushed. Not buried.

Swallowed.

The shaft mouth was sealed in haste.

The company moved on.

Coal Hollow withered down to mold and ruin.

But something stayed behind.

And it wasn't just the rotting boney dumps, either.

**The Whistler in the Rock**

The old ones who lingered said the dead never gave up clawing at the dark.

Some nights — when the rain bled from the hills and the dirt sweated rust — a sound would crawl up from the buried seams.

A high, slow, singsong whistle, broken and wrong.

It reeked like death trapped in an attic — thick and sweet like syrup poured over something rotting.

It wasn't the wind.

It wasn't a bird.

It was a tune — half a lullaby, half a funeral dirge — slithering out of the earth, wet and putrid.

Those who heard it said their hair bristled. Their teeth ached as if roots were being tugged from the jaw.

Some said the whistling wasn't just sound—it was a thing, something slick and hollow, forcing its way up through the rock, clawing blind for the world above.

A boy once leaned in to listen at the old shaft cap.

By morning, they found him staggering among the slag piles, bleeding thick and black from both ears, the tune dribbling out of his cracked lips like drool.

His eyes were open wide and empty, seeing nothing but the tunnels he couldn't crawl out of anymore.

He never spoke again — but sometimes at night, if the wind hit right, folks swore they could hear him whistling it too.

### The Warning of Coal Hollow

The last hands left in Coal Hollow scrawled a warning on the warped walls of the abandoned shanties:

If you hear the whistling, don't whistle back.

If the ground breathes against your skin, turn back.

And if the tune ever creeps onto your tongue, bury it deep — or it'll dig you down with it.

Because some graves don't stay shut.

Some songs don't want saving.

Some just want a throat to climb into.

# The Telltale Lilac Bush

The Tygart Valley River snakes 135 miles from the Alleghenies to the Monongahela, its waters curling past Beverly, Grafton, and towns too small to claim a map.

But between Union and Lillian, there was once a dirt road that no one travels anymore.

If you stumble upon it, you'll think it's just a deer path—choked with nettles, veined with roots, its old wagon ruts filled with water like sockets without eyes. There's almost nothing left.

Just some broken porcelain teeth from teacups.

The glint of a green bottle like a half-buried eye.

And a lilac bush that refuses to die.

It stands there, bold and blooming, long after the house that kept it is just rot and stone.

And beneath its roots, the ground still remembers.

## A House Full of Hate

They say an old couple lived there, not kindly.

He was sour. She was sharper. The neighbors said their bickering could boil creek water. They hadn't shared a meal in peace for twenty years.

So, when she disappeared, no one was surprised.

Not really.

Some muttered that the old man had done what many had long suspected he'd always wanted to do. But there was no body. Just whispers and an empty chair.

He lived well enough after that. Too well.

Started hosting card games and corn liquor socials. Laughed harder than a man who lost a wife should.

Until the afternoon, the men came to talk.

*Tap-Tap-Tap*

They were just sipping cider and swapping lies at his kitchen table when it started.

*Tap. Tap. Tap.*

The windowpane twitched like something was knocking.

Not a branch. Not the wind. Something more intentional.

*Tap. Tap. Tap.*

They all looked.

*Tap. Tap. Tap.*

The lilac bush out front was moving—its branches shifting like fingers, tapping the glass like knuckles on a coffin lid. One long stem curled against the pane and slowly drew back, waving like a hand.

Beckoning.

The old man chuckled. "Just the wind," he said.

But his voice cracked like kindling.

And the men—curious and uneasy—rose.

They stepped outside.

## What They Dug

The lilac waved again.

 No wind.

Just a sick rhythm to its sway, like it knew they were watching.

One man touched the base of the bush.

Another began to dig.

The dirt was soft. Damp.

It came up easy. Too easy.

Then someone gasped.

Another fell to his knees.

And one of them swore he heard the bush sigh.

Because beneath it, a hand emerged.

Delicate. Swollen. Pale. Rotted.

And curling between the knuckles like a vine,

the lilac's root twisted up from the palm,

feeding on what was left of her.

**The River Took Him**

The old man screamed. Then he ran.

He didn't grab his coat. Didn't take the path.

He went straight to the river and never came back out.

They say the current took him. Or the mud did.

Or maybe the thing in the dirt followed him down.

**The Lilac Remains**

They never replanted the bush.

They didn't have to.

It still grows there, full and bright and wrong.

Each spring, it blooms violet and thick, and the breeze that moves its branches smells faintly like earth and old breath.

Locals say if you pass by at dusk, you might hear a woman sobbing beneath the petals.

Or worse—laughing.

And if the bush starts to wave?

You'd best not wave back.

Because sometimes the dead don't want to be found.

But the things growing out of them do.

# The Unsettled Grave of Morris Haggerty

No stone. No name. Just dirt that won't stay still.

There once was a grave—a ragged, sour little mound of earth tucked near the edge of West Liberty, just off the old road, where grass grows patchy and the wind forgets how to blow. It was marked only by a few broken stones, one at the head, one at the foot, like someone was trying to remember how graves are supposed to look.

But no name. No cross. No flowers.

Because the man buried there—Morris Haggerty, an old Irish peddler with crooked teeth and a bent spine—wasn't supposed to be found.

Dead.

## The Murder

In 1853, Haggerty made the mistake of trusting the wrong soul. He traveled with a satchel of cheap wares—buttons, ribbons, and things not worth killing for, but still, he died for them.

His body was not buried by a family but by someone trying to hide it.

The grave was shallow.

The soil turned sloppy with decay.

They say the killer buried him in the dark—facedown, hands broken, coins still in his boots.

## The Nights After

It should have ended there.

Rot, silence, and forgetting.

But something never settled in that grave. Not long after, strange lights began to flicker above it.

Not lanterns. Not fireflies. But cold glimmers, floating low like eyes watching through a veil.

Then came the noises.

Scraping.

Snarling.

Whimpering.

And then, the sound of feet dancing—but wrong. Too fast. Too frantic. Like something in pain, trying to shake out its own bones.

**The Capering Ghost**

One night, the *thing* climbed from its dirt bed. A shriveled figure in tattered burial clothes, its mouth wide open as if still screaming, its hands twitching, still groping for something stolen. It staggered through the dark, dragging filth and maggots behind it until it reached the house of Doctor Thornley.

What it did inside was not silent.

It filched a knife from the kitchen.

Ripped undergarments from a bureau.

Tossed silverware to the floor, one piece at a time, as if trying to match a sound it once heard during his murder.

And all the while, the doctor stood paralyzed in his hallway, watching as the peddler's ghost twitched like a hooked fish, capering around the home, searching for the hands that slit his throat.

**No Justice. Just Fear.**

The town learned quickly. They avoided the grave.

They whispered of mistaken vengeance, how Haggerty was likely searching for his killer, and how he might mistake any of them for the man who put him in the ground like a rotted dog.

No one went near the mound.

No one stayed near the doctor's house after sundown.

And no one ever confessed.

But some say if you pass that stretch of earth now—especially in November when the ground freezes soft and shallow—you can see something standing up behind the stones.

It's gaunt.

It's sodden.

And it's still holding the knife it stole.

He isn't looking for peace.

He's looking for the last face he ever saw.

And God help you if you look like him.

Or even something close.

# Devil at the White Raven Inn

It happened near midnight, sometime in the early 1900s, when the White Raven Inn—just a crooked-roofed roadhouse tucked down a dead-end hollow—was pulsing with music, liquor, and wild laughter. There were around thirty souls packed tight into the pine-planked room. Boot heels beat against the floorboards, tankards clanged, and the fiddle screamed as if the strings were soaked in blood. The place smelled of woodsmoke, corn whiskey, and sweat. Windows fogged from within. Doors rattled from the stamping feet.

## Then the Devil Showed

And that's when the air shifted.

It came all at once— a gasp of silence like the breath of the room had been snatched away.

Then the floor cracked.

Not a simple groan of old lumber, but a splitting, loud and sharp, like the world beneath had been struck with an axe.

And from the wound in the wood, *he* rose.

A thing black as burnt bone, hooved and horned, its skin slick with ash and heat. His eyes were hot nails driven into his skull, glowing red. A sulfur stench poured from the opening as he hovered—not walked—around the stunned crowd, feet never touching the floor.

He smiled, a wide animal grin full of cracked teeth and black gums.

And then he danced.

Not like the others.

His dance mocked theirs—wild and jerking, limbs too long, hips snapping, arms swinging in unnatural circles as if pulled by invisible strings. His cloven feet struck sparks with every step. With one crack of his tail against the wall, a blast of flame shot from the spot where it struck, burning the plaster and revealing something moving inside it—something with too many eyes.

People screamed.

Some tried to run, but the doors wouldn't budge. Others dropped to their knees, hands clamped over their ears, eyes rolled back white.

The devil's grin grew wider.

Then—just as quick—he plunged back into the floor, the boards snapping shut behind him with the sound of clapping thunder.

### They All Went Home Changed

The music never played again.

Afterward, the dancers staggered home through the woods, their laughter gone. Some swore off drink.

Others took to carrying Bibles with shaking hands.

A few disappeared entirely, and one woman—still in her dress shoes—was found days later walking in circles in a dry creek bed, whispering, "He danced too..."

The White Raven Inn was abandoned.

The mark from his tail still burns black into the wall, and nothing—paint, plaster, or prayer—will cover it.

And if you pass by that hollow after midnight, sometimes, you can hear the fiddle shriek all by itself.

And the sound of hooves-*clack, clack, clack.*

# Mamie of 22 Mine Road

### A Body in the Brush

On Wednesday, June 22, 1932, a berry-picker in the hills above Logan made a grisly discovery in a tangle of brush on Trace Mountain. She lay facedown in the weeds, soaked from the storms that had rolled over the mountain the night before. A woman in a blue cotton dress dotted with white polka dots, with one red shoe still on her foot. Her hat was found tossed thirty feet away as though it had been flung in a final, frantic moment. She was broken.

The bruises over her eye were deep and purple-black. Her neck had been snapped. There were powder burns on her cheek. Two shots to the head.

And then, the killer had slit her throat.

This was not a quiet death. It was rage.

### The Woman Beneath the Choir Robe

The woman was identified as Mamie Thurman, age thirty-one, a housewife and churchgoer, married to Logan city patrolman Jack Thurman, a man seventeen years her senior. She sang in the choir. She attended every service. But Mamie kept secrets that clung to her like perfume and smoke.

### Blood on the Bookman's Hands

Police found blood in the home and vehicle of Harry Robertson, her landlord. He was no criminal on paper—bookish, bespectacled, with a quiet voice and a respectable reputation. But he admitted to the affair easily. Claimed it had lasted two years. Claimed she had others too. Mamie was seen with several prominent men, and Robertson's friend and handyman, Clarence Stephenson, had driven him to and from those clandestine meetings in the woods.

Stephenson was the one they charged.

Not Harry. Never Harry.

### A Conviction Without Closure

Stephenson insisted he was innocent, but the jury didn't believe him. In 1934, he was sentenced to life in prison. He died behind bars at Huttonsville eight years later. No one ever proved who killed Mamie Thurman.

But Mamie never forgot.

And she never left the mountain.

They say her ghost wanders 22 Mine Road.

## Mamie Walks the Mountain Still

Coal truck drivers have seen her standing in the middle of the road, pale and soaked, one red shoe tapping slowly on the gravel. Sometimes, she asks for a ride. They pull over. Let her in. But by the time they reach the bottom of the mountain, the seat is empty.

Others have reported screams echoing through the trees. A gunshot. The sound of a woman choking. It doesn't come from any house or hollow—only from the dark.

## Proof in the Powder

Some swear there's a spot near the place where she was found where, if you stop your car and put it in neutral, it will roll uphill. They say it's her, pushing you to safety—or dragging you back to where she died. To test it, people coat their bumpers in baby powder. When the car stops, they check.

And they find handprints.

Small. Delicate.

Pressed in tight.

Mamie Thurman may be buried, but her bones don't rest easy.

Not in that mountain.

Not on that road.

And not in the minds of those who left her behind.

# "Where's My Head?"

## The Farm by Mount Harmony

There was an old farm near Mount Harmony, a forsaken place sold for pennies—and rightly so, for something awful lingered in its bones. Mister Salters, practical and dismissive of superstition, bought the land and moved into the weathered farmhouse. But each night when the moon rose full and pale, precisely at 8:30, a ghastly voice thundered through the night air:

"Where is my head?"

Salters searched the farm, lantern trembling in hand, eyes wide, breath steaming like ghostly whispers. The source eluded him, a spectral echo that seemed everywhere yet nowhere at once. On the next full moon, as the silver disk hung bloated and ominous, the voice returned, deeper, colder, dripping with decay:

"Where is my head?"

This time, as Salters crept toward the old, abandoned well, the voice rose clearer, foul with rot:

"Down here—in the well."

## Jealousy and Madness

Long ago, a young couple named Mary and Tom Dixon lived on that very farm. Mary was fair and lively, Tom handsome and strong. Many men coveted Mary's affection, but her heart belonged only to Tom. Among the rejected, one festered darkly—Jack Wilson, a man twisted and vile who never washed and wore tattered clothes stained with sweat and soil. His eyes glittered like a rabid animal's, wild and reckless, always spying on Mary as she worked, whispering curses under his sour breath. Jack Wilson was cruelty itself, kicking small kittens that crossed his path, nursing grudges until they became festering wounds of rage.

## Blood and Scythe

One humid day in Fairmont, Wilson spotted Mary alone. Dark visions clouded his mind; he sprinted to the ferry, crossed into Palatine, and followed the dusty road leading to Mount Harmony. Breathless, sweating, and crazed, he fetched a hidden scythe from the tangled shadows of the woods.

Wilson crept to the Dixon farm, scythe gleaming cruelly. Tom Dixon, unaware, hoed corn beneath the sweltering sun. Dixon's dog barked fiercely, alerting him. He turned, eyes wide with terror, to see Wilson charging, mouth twisted into a raving snarl, blade swinging like death itself.

Tom bolted toward the farmhouse, Wilson gaining swiftly, scythe whistling through the air. Nearing the well, Tom stumbled, heart pounding.

Wilson lunged—but Tom wrestled fiercely, grappling for the scythe.

They struggled furiously, dirt and blood mingling beneath their feet. Finally, in a desperate swing, Tom severed Wilson's head.

Blood sprayed thick and black, splattering Tom's face and hands.

## He Tossed the Head in the Well

Wilson's head rolled sickeningly, a grim orb tumbling down into the murky darkness of the well.

Terrified and guilt-ridden, Tom dragged the headless corpse deep into the woods, burying it hastily beneath thick brambles. He slaughtered a young pig, hurling its carcass into the well, fouling the water to hide his sin.

## The Lingering Horror

Days turned into weeks. Wilson, always strange and repulsive, was scarcely missed. Yet whispers rustled among the trees, dread seeped from the earth itself. Tom Dixon grew gaunt and hollow-eyed, Mary aged prematurely, skin wan and eyes hollow. Abruptly, they fled westward, vanishing forever.

Every new tenant that tried to inhabit the cursed farmhouse soon heard the dreadful nightly refrain:

"Where is my head?"

And always, the chilling answer echoed:

"Down here—in the well."

One by one, they fled, abandoning hearth and home to ruin.

Mister Salters himself eventually yielded, fleeing the haunting echoes.

Now, the farmhouse rots, reclaimed by shadows. The old well is buried beneath earth and heavy stones, yet the ghastly voice persists, muffled but eternal, whispering to unlucky passersby beneath the moon's malevolent glow:

"Where is my head?"

# Eaton Tunnel: The Mountain Took Them

## The Line That Cut Through Stone

In 1851, the Northwestern Virginia Railroad of the B&O carved its intention through the wilderness—103 miles of iron and promise, stretching from Grafton to Parkersburg. They called it the Parkersburg Branch, which threaded through the hills like a knife, burrowing beneath them in 23 tunnels.

One of those tunnels would take more than its share.

It began as Eaton Tunnel—a proud artery of progress, completed in 1853 and christened with sweat and stone. But over time, as names and maps changed, the stories stayed. And the bodies never left.

### The Ground Beneath Was Never Still

The deaths began almost immediately.

- January 1854, a man was crushed by a rockfall. His name was lost, but the sound of stone cracking bone still echoes.

- January 8, 1855, Terry Duffy was yanked skyward by a hook that caught his coat. He rose like a puppet, screaming, before being dashed against the pit's shaft, falling 125 feet to his death.

- August 22, 1865, another rockfall—three men buried alive in silence.

- November 1866, cholera swept through the camp. In four days, fifteen dead, their bodies stacked in shallow graves before the frost took the rest.

- February 1867, the tunnel opened wide again—three more crushed beneath tons of shale.

- 1877, five drifters, asleep in a stolen boxcar, were ground to a pulp when a train wrecked in the dark mouth of the tunnel.

- March 1890, a man named Simpson—hit head-on by a locomotive, his remains found smeared on stones.

- October 1907, brakeman H.J. Garletz tried to jump trains, missed, and was dragged beneath the wheels.

Every few years, the tunnel drank deep.

## June 6, 1963

A century later, Eaton Tunnel still stood, weary and worn. Crews arrived in the 1960s to widen it. Strengthen it. But the mountain had heard enough. That morning, drills chewed at the rock, and men shouted over the clamor. Then came the collapse.

A roar like judgment. Dust and stone and screams.

They pulled Author Boggs, 24, from the rubble—his body shattered, his breath shallow. He died days later.

Harry "Buck" Nichols was never found.

Some say the tunnel crushed him completely. Others believe something older, darker, took him in that moment—something that lives where sunlight never touches. His body was never recovered.

The tunnel became his tomb.

## Buried But Not Forgotten

The work stopped. They sealed the tunnel like a grave and left it to rot. The forest closed around it, thick with vines and silence.

A second tunnel was carved beside it, and for a while, the trains still came. But not for long.

## Now they call it Lost Tunnel.

Its walls crumble. Black mold blooms like decay. And the air inside is sharp—unnatural, heavy with breath not your own. In June, the shifting stone sounds like footsteps. And sometimes—a lantern flickers in the dark, swinging, held by no hand you can see.

Some say it's the dead. Trying to get out.

Or leading others in.

## The Mouth That Still Breathes

Those who dare enter don't stay long.

They return pale, trembling. They speak of a metallic stench—of whispers beneath the ground and the sensation of something crawling along the ceiling just above their heads.

The entrance is blocked now.

Boulders carefully placed keep curious feet at bay.

But those who know the land will tell you—that tunnel was never empty.

And whatever stirs in the dark... it's not finished yet.

# Lake Shawnee Amusement Park

### The Land That Should Never Have Been Disturbed

Before the laughter. Before the rusted ticket booths and the broken rides.

There was blood.

And it was children who spilled it.

In 1783, at the edge of the woods and along the sluggish bend of the river, the Clay children died screaming.

Tabitha Clay — no more than ten — fought like a wild thing to keep the hatchet from her brother's scalp.

They tore into her with knives, stabbing her again and again until the dirt drank her small life away.

Bartley Clay was shot in the chest.

He crawled in the mud for hours before he stopped.

Their youngest brother, Ezekiel, was dragged away into the trees.

They burned him alive.

They buried what was left of the children in shallow, angry graves.

The land did not forget.

It festered. It hungered.

**A Park Built on Suffering**

By 1926, the Clay children's names were already dust.

Forgotten by the living.

But not by the ground.

Conley Snidow, Sr. built a children's amusement park right over their graves.

A Ferris wheel.

A swimming pool.

A circle of swings.

The land tolerated the noise for a while.

But blood remembers blood.

And soon it began to take again.

In 1927, Emiline Shrader — hair in ribbons, laughing under the wide sky — was crushed beneath a truck as it backed toward the swings.

Witnesses said she didn't even scream.

Her small body hit the earth like a broken doll.

Later, George Wythe — a boy with big dreams and a hand-me-down swimsuit — drowned in the park's pool.

Pulled down by something no one could see.

His legs battered bloody against the drain grates until he didn't struggle anymore.

The laughter curdled.

The rides slowed.

Lake Shawnee Amusement Park was abandoned to the weeds and the rot.

But the land was not finished.

**The Bones Beneath**

In the 1980s, Gaylord White tried to resurrect the park.

He sent bulldozers into the ground.

The earth did not welcome them.

First came bones.

Hundreds of them.

Children's teeth still curled in broken jaws.

Tiny skulls smashed and crumbling.

Beads and arrowheads tangled in the roots.

They found a forgotten Shawnee burial ground.

No one counted how many bodies they disturbed before they stopped digging.

By then, the dead were already awake.

And they were angry.

**The Ghosts That Refuse to Leave**

The land is wrong now.

Thick and heavy like a mouth full of mud.

Visitors see shapes flickering between the trees.

They hear the old chains creaking when the air is still.

Sometimes, they glimpse a girl standing by the broken swings — a child soaked in blood, her head canted sideways like her neck cannot hold it up.

Those who stay too long hear the laughter.

Not the kind of laughter that belongs to the living.

The kind that belongs to things that should never have been disturbed.

Some say you can still visit Lake Shawnee today.

They call it abandoned.

But it is not empty.

The Clay children are still there.

The Shawnee bones are still there.

And something older still curls beneath the soil, older than language, older than light.

It waits.

And if you step too close to the swings at dusk—you'll hear it.

Not laughter.

Not weeping.

Only the slow, hungry groan of chains.

And something moving, just beneath the dirt, reaching for you—touching you—following you home.

# Booger Hole

**Booger Hole: The Place That Ate Its Dead**

Deep in the choked hollows of Big Otter and Rush Fork, there's a place no map can warn you about properly.

They call it Booger Hole.

Ask six old folks why, and you'll get six stories, all worse than the last. Some say it's the gut of the woods — black, hungry, and swallowing farms whole.

Some say it's where the Bogyman made his home — because back then, the woods weren't just thick; they were bloodthirsty.

Booger Hole was packed tight with hard men and harder women — the Cottrells, the Lyons, the Boggses, the Joneses, the Moores.

Good with a plow.

Better with a shotgun.

But something in that soil turned on them.

Something ancient, maybe. Or maybe just the rot in their own bones.

Between the late 1800s and 1917, Booger Hole became a place where people disappeared like smoke.

No search parties.

No bodies.

Just blood drying on stones and whispers rising with the mist.

### Murder Begets Murder

In 1883, Andrew "Andy" Hargis—stonemason, drunkard, unlucky soul—set off down the road with $300 in his pocket and never came home.

Folks say his aunt, Margaret Moore, bought that death with stolen pension money. They say someone slit him open and buried him under the belly of the hills, deep where the worms don't even wander.

1897, Joseph Clark—a watchmaker with nimble fingers—slept at the Booger Hole schoolhouse.

Come morning, he was gone.

All they found was a slick trail of blood that led to the creek and then just...stopped.

1899, Louis Cohen—a dirt-poor farmer—murdered. No one cared enough to remember how.

That same year, Lacy Ann Boggs—74 years old and who some called a witch—was shot in the back while rocking on her porch, smoking her pipe and telling stories to her granddaughter.

Her body stayed there all night, eyes wide open, mouth sagging, an apple still clutched in her hand.

The child never left her side.

Too scared to move.

Too scared to scream.

They said Lacy knew too much.

Knew who buried Andy Hargis.

Knew where the bones twisted under the roots.

Maybe she cursed the ones who killed her — cursed them to dream of bridle bits in their mouths, dragonflies stinging their flesh, forced to crawl like animals through poison oak and briars.

Marshall Cottrell swore he did. Swore he flew like a bird to her grave every night in his sleep.

But still, no one was ever punished.

Booger Hole has its ways of hiding things.

**The Ground Eats Its Own**

In 1902, John Newman, a Swedish peddler carrying a sack of cash, took a wrong turn.

Blood spattered between the house and the barn where he vanished.

They killed a colt over the same bloody spot to mask the stain.

It didn't fool anyone.

But it didn't save him either.

Then 1917 came — and with it, fire.

Preston Tanner and his young wife, Osie, were fresh blood, newly planted in Booger Hole's foul soil.

While Osie was away, the neighbors—David "Andrew" Sampson and his son Howard—paid Preston a visit.

Played dominoes.

Then crushed Preston's skull with a clawhammer and set the house aflame, letting the fire gnaw his body until it cracked and crumbled.

In the ashes, they found the blackened frame of a man and an empty can of lamp oil melted to his ribs.

Howard Sampson was sweet on Osie.

Sweet enough to kill.

Sweet enough to lie.

Sweet enough to make the dead weep under their shallow graves.

## The Grand Jury and the Booger Hole Mob

The Clay County Courthouse tried to hold Booger Hole still.

Tried to hammer truth from blood and bone.

But the dirt was deeper than any shovel could dig.

Witnesses babbled, old women whispered, and Caroline Moore — trembling under the eyes of the law — finally confessed:

Wrapped and trapped in a sheet, she was forced to listen to her brother, James Fletcher Moore, and her brother-in-law, John Lyons, dragging Andy Hargis's dead weight back to their house.

She chewed her way out just in time to see them bury the body under the floorboards.

Later, they dug him up, burned him, and buried him again—deeper.

Detectives clawed into the ground where the house once stood and pulled up burnt hair, cufflinks stamped "A.H.," and a whetstone with HARGIS scratched deep into it.

James and John stood trial.

Not guilty.

Of course.

The mob had its own verdict.

They dynamited the homes tied to the murders — blew them into kindling — and tacked handbills to what was left:

"We declare that the people have waited patiently for the law to remedy Booger Hole. We will now do the work the law has failed to do. If it becomes necessary to burn every house and kill every resident in this community, we will do so. Justice will be served."

After that, the woods grew quiet.

At least, quiet enough.

**The Things That Still Walk**

Booger Hole's ghosts are not quiet.

They do not drift like smoke.

They cling to the ground—screaming, sobbing, scratching at the roots. One boy, squirrel rifle slung over his shoulder, stumbled upon a woman once—a woman in a white dress that dragged the dirt.

Her hair was black and filthy, tangled all the way to the ground.

She staggered toward him, hands covering her face, wailing a sound so broken it bent the trees.

He waited, thinking she was just some moonshiner's wife, mad with grief.

He thought he'd cough or shuffle his boots when she got close.

But she never saw him. Never touched him.

She lifted straight into the air—face still hidden, mouth still open—and disappeared. And the boy ran all the way home, screaming louder than any ghost.

The bad folks might be gone from Booger Hole.

But the dead never packed up and left.

Some say the earth itself remembers.

Some say the worst of them — the liars, the killers, the ones who smiled as they swung the hammer—still slip through the trees when the moon is high.

Coming back to see what's left of their work.

On still nights, the living hear them.

Whispers in the timber. Footsteps in the hollow.

The smell of burnt hair and old blood hanging in the air.

Folks who know better leave Booger Hole well enough alone.

Because out there, in the black woods, it's hard to tell the good from the bad.

And harder still to tell the living from the dead.

# Coffin Rider of Booths Creek

Missus Hess Bender, a stout, plain woman from Bobtown, Pennsylvania, had never put much stock in ghost stories. But that changed one muggy summer evening when she took the long road home through the Fairmont area, following the winding stretch of Booths Creek Road.

She stopped at the Smiths' for a drink—sweat on her brow, shoes caked with dust. They welcomed her in, fed her supper, and sent her off just as twilight smeared its blood-red bruise across the sky.

Only thirty minutes later, she was back, bonnetless, trembling.

She said she'd forgotten her bonnet, but that was a lie.

Out on the lonely road, just past the bend where the creek twists through the trees, she'd seen something that turned her spine to glass. A ghostly coffin—long, wooden, and upright—rose straight up from the dirt in the center of the road like a rotten tooth breaking through gums. Sitting on top was a man, pale and stiff, his face slack as wax, eyes wide and unblinking. It drifted up to her height, hovered... then silently drifted over the creek's edge and vanished into the darkness below.

She dared not cross its path. She ran.

### It Came Again

Years passed, but the thing returned.

Old Isaac Koon, a farmer living nearby, saw it next. He came home white as a shroud, muttering about the floating box and the dead man on top. Then came two women from Bobtown. Then more. One by one, neighbors swore they'd seen it too—always at the same time of night, always rising from the same cursed patch of earth. It would lift from the upper side of the road, glide across, and vanish over the bank like it was following some deathly, silent path.

### A Dare in the Dark

One dusky evening, a group of boys from Monongah and Rhea Chapel had stayed late after a baseball game in Boothsville. Though a new road had been cut up the creek, they chose the old road—shorter but fouler with old stories.

Tom Rhea rode slightly ahead of Barney Whaling and Will Barnes. One of the boys scoffed as they passed the dreaded curve:

"I wish I could see him," he said. "I'd whistle for him to dance."

He shouldn't have said that.

No sooner had the words left his mouth than the road seemed to open like a freshly cut wound. The coffin erupted from the earth, the man atop it motionless, mouth agape, eyes full of midnight. One of the horses screamed and jumped—twelve feet in the air, wild with terror. Tom barely stayed in the saddle. Barney and Will froze, watching the coffin glide across the dirt like it had wheels beneath it, cross the road, and melt into the darkness over the bank.

## The Bullet That Wouldn't Rest

The ghost's story goes like this:

During April and May of 1863, Confederate Generals William Jones and John Imboden led a raid through West Virginia. Their aim: disrupt the Baltimore and Ohio Railroad, gather cattle, and bleed the land of supplies. On April 12, 1863, the raiders swept through Fairmont.

In the chaos, a Union soldier shot a Confederate in the leg. The man was caught and tossed into a prison wagon. But he never made it. A Union captain recognized him as the one who had shot his brother and, without a word, raised his pistol and blew the soldier's brains out.

The body was stuffed in a crude pine coffin and buried hastily up a sloping bank beside Booths Creek Road. No marker. No prayer. Just cold earth.

The killer would come to regret it.

Years later, that same Union officer settled in Monongah and fell for a girl in Watson. To see her, he had to ride that cursed road—right past the place where he'd spilled blood during the war.

One night, the ground groaned.

His horse reared, eyes rolling white. From the dark belly of the hillside came a low, hateful moan. And then it appeared: the dead soldier, skin drawn tight over a grinning skull, uniform rotting, slumped atop his risen coffin.

The captain turned white, dug heels into his horse, and fled. But it didn't end. Each time he went to visit the girl, the ghost returned—riding his box, trailing rot and vengeance. Friends scoffed. Laughed.

Until the soldier didn't come back.

They found him sprawled in a ditch near the old road. A bullet through his skull.

When curious townsfolk dug up the Confederate's grave, they found the coffin opened. The corpse still clutched a smoking pistol in skeletal fingers. There was no bullet in his body. No exit wound. Only that rancid grin and empty eyes.

The bullet had found its way home. But not so, the ghost.

**Still There**

The road's mostly forgotten now. Grass grows in the cracks. Cars roar past on newer paths, drivers unaware of the terror that haunts that shallow stretch.

But the ground remembers. And some nights, when the wind smells of an oncoming storm, and the moon is low and yet to be consumed by clouds...

He comes back.

The rider on the coffin.

Drifting.

Waiting.

Looking for someone to follow him down into the dark.

Or hunt them down like the one who killed him.

# The Ghost of Gamble Run

## A Man Named John Gamble Vanished

In November of 1850, a man named John Gamble vanished from the banks of the Ohio River. He was thirty-six, a carpenter, a cider-maker, and a father. And he was carrying nearly two hundred dollars in cash—his life's work folded into small green slips tucked neatly in his coat pocket. That day, he'd tied off his skiff near New Martinsville, barrels stacked like bones in a cart, and took the muddy path up the hillside to collect a debt from the Whiteman brothers.

## Leban Mercer

With him was Leban Mercer—a quiet man, rough around the edges, who'd been owed a few dollars by Gamble himself.

Witnesses say Mercer left the Whiteman farm soaked to the knees, shirt clinging with sweat, at two in the morning. They say it hadn't rained.

They also say he suddenly had money in his pockets he hadn't had the day before.

Gamble's boat was found drifting, empty. His barrels bobbed gently in the current.

And Gamble? Gone—swallowed by the hills, by the black of the earth.

Rumors curdled. Whispers spread like mold in a damp room. But without a body, no noose could be tied.

Until the dead man spoke.

## John Hindman Meets a Ghost

A year later, after the corn harvest, there was a husking bee—a wild one full of laughter and whiskey. At the end of the night, young men raced each other home through the dark hills near Point Pleasant Creek, kicking up dead leaves as they scattered like rats into the woods.

One of them, John Hindman, took a path along Ray's Run. Alone. Or so he thought.

As he walked, a figure appeared beside him.

Pale. Hollow-eyed.

"I believe you do not know me, sir," it said.

Hindman stopped cold. "No," he answered, heart pounding. "I don't."

"I am John Gamble. Leban Mercer killed me. Take him up and have justice done."

The *thing* said more—grisly things.

Things that chilled the marrow and carved themselves into Hindman's bones.

Then, the figure vanished. Gone. No prints. No breath.

Just the wind and the wide-eyed moon.

Hindman, a skeptic by nature, said nothing—until the dreams came. Until he woke choking on phantom water. Until he couldn't hold the secret any longer.

He told close friends. Described Gamble's clothes exactly. Clothes no living man could have known.

**Leban Mercer Walked Free**

And still—Leban Mercer walked free.

Until Hindman, clever and quiet, lured him into conversation. Drew truths from him only a killer would know—truths the ghost had whispered in that cold field.

A warrant was signed. Mercer was tried. Witnesses came forward—boys who saw the two men together that night, a man who found a grave-shaped dent in the mud by the creek, black hair poking from the soil.

Mercer's roommate swore the man cried out in his sleep: "Damn you, Gamble, I'll take that money!"

Mercer had the promissory note, too—the one Gamble was last seen holding.

Still… it wasn't enough. Leban Mercer walked.

But the creek where Gamble's body was likely dumped took his name.

**Gamble Run.**

And those who walk its banks say that when the moon is high, and the fields rot sweet with cider apples, you can still see a figure drift up from the creekbed.

His mouth opens in a scream no one hears.

And if you walk too close… he'll tell you how he died.

And he won't stop talking until someone finally listens.

# The Devil and Mister Webb

### It Happened in Lost Creek

This is the tale of something old, something whispered—something that clawed its way out of winter's throat and left blood on the snow.

It happened around Lost Creek, on the road that would one day be called Lost Creek-Lomines Mill Road, some two and a half miles east of town. The year was in the early 1800s, long before pavement and light, when the woods were thick and unkind, and the dark could swallow a man whole.

A man named Webb lived near where Liberty Church now rots, empty and silent. He was known for two things: drinking hard and talking harder. That winter was bitter. Ice hung from the eaves. Trees groaned beneath frost. And Webb, drunk on applejack and pride, filled a tin coffee pot with liquor and staggered toward the door.

He paused before leaving, silhouetted by the hearth light, and said to his kin around the fire: "I am going out to fight the Devil."

Then he stepped into the night.

**The Devil Answered**

No one thought much of it. Webb rambled when drunk. But morning came, and Webb didn't return.

A search began. It was cold. The sun couldn't cut the fog. They found his trail along the creek—staggering boot prints weaving between the trees. They followed it down a hill, across a frozen stream, and into a hollow.

That's where they found him.

Or what was left.

Webb's body was leaned up under a hickory tree, arms slack at his sides. His face had been twisted in terror—jaw shattered, mouth open in a silent scream. His torso was flayed, and ribs cracked open like firewood. His guts were pulled from his belly and scattered in the snow like red worms frozen in mid-squirm.

Something had ripped him apart. Not eaten. Not clawed. Torn. Like a doll.

Beside him, untouched, was the coffee pot.

Still upright.

Cold. Its contents empty.

Tipped slightly to the right.

Nobody ever found tracks. No bear. No cat. No man. Just Webb and the coffee pot and the long, dead silence of winter.

People say he did what he promised—went out to fight the Devil.

And the Devil came.

Some nights, when the wind howls just right down Lost Creek-Lomines Mill Road, folks swear they hear something gurgling in the trees, something wet, something heavy, dragging bones across the frozen leaves.

And some say that if you find the old hickory and stand beneath it long enough, a hand will offer you a cold drink from a tin pot.

But do not drink it.

Because Mister Webb did.

And then he met the Devil.

# Three Black Cats

### A Lost Road

Once upon a time, in the hollers of West Virginia, a circuit-riding preacher made his rounds, traveling church to church on his gray mare, spreading the Word to the scattered flocks. One evening, as the wind picked up, a hint of snow hit the air, and the clouds rolled in.

The preacher was old and chilled, and his bones ached. He found himself wishing he was home more than preaching, so he turned the mare around and started for his house.

He chose not to preach at the church this week and would catch them up on the Bible verses next week. But along the way, he got lost in the woods and far from home. Thunder rumbled like the belly of something awfully big and awfully hungry. The trees swayed and whispered. Still, he whispered back to himself, "The Lord will take care of me."

Then, a light.

### The Haunted Offer

It flickered from a distant cabin. He rode up and knocked. A man opened the door.

"Preacher, I'd take you in," he said, "but this cabin's tight—wife and kids already sleeping."

The preacher sagged, wet, and weary. "Well," he sighed, "the Lord will take care of me."

"Hold on," the man called after him. "There's the old big house up yonder. Nobody stays there. You can sleep by the hearth. But preacher—"

"Yes?"

"It's haunted."

The preacher tipped his hat. "The Lord will take care of me."

He put up his horse in the barn, stepped into the grand old house, and found a roaring hearth laid ready. He lit a lamp, settled into a chair, and read from his Bible, the fire popping and hissing like old bones.

Hours passed. Then… a sound.

### Cats and Coals

A soft thump. A scratching.

From the corner crept a cat. Black as coal. Eyes like twin green lanterns. It stretched, stepped into the red-hot coals, and rolled like a pig in a wallow.

Then it sat at the preacher's feet and hissed: "Wait till Emmett comes."

The preacher cleared his throat and turned the page.

Another thump. Another scratch.

A second cat. Bigger than the first. Big as a dog.

It, too, wallowed in the coals, then sat at the other foot.

"Now, what shall we do with him?" it asked.

The first replied, "Wait till Emmett comes."

The preacher clutched his Bible tighter.

Then—a roar. The floor shook.

From the shadows came a third cat. Blacker than night, big as a calf. It snarled, chewed the coals, spat fire, and sat directly in front of the old man.

"What shall we do with him?" it growled.

"Wait till Emmett comes." the others replied.

**When Emmett Comes**

The preacher stood up slowly, shut his Bible with a snap, and cleared his throat. "Well now," he said, "I surely appreciate the hospitality... But when Emmett comes, you tell him—" He backed to the door, wide-eyed, voice cracking—"—you tell him I been here, and I done left."

He mounted that gray mare like he was twenty years younger and rode off so fast the wind couldn't catch him.

He never rode through those woods again. And they say he never missed preaching a Sunday after that.

# The Hitchhiking Ghost

## A Night Too Cold

Three teenage boys were riding home on a frigid West Virginia night many years ago. Their car had no heat. The headlights were dim, and the snow battered the windshield like gravel. The tires, balding and thin, groaned beneath them. It was past curfew, but they dared not to go faster—the roads were icy, the night treacherous. Laughter broke the tension when one of the boys cracked a joke. But then they fell silent. Something moved in the snow. Crawling. On hands and knees.

The driver slammed the brakes. The car skidded to a stop. They jumped out, crunching over snow. A girl lay in the road, frostbitten hands trembling, feet bare and blue, a deep, glistening gash carved into her forehead. Dried blood rimmed her scalp, her eyes glassy and lost.

They rushed her into the back seat.

She shook uncontrollably.

"I just want to go home," she whispered.

**Get Me to Mason's Lawn**

At first, she wouldn't tell them where she lived. Then came the breathless plea:

"Get me to Mason's Lawn. Before it's too late."

She passed out cold.

One boy wrapped a bandanna around a wound on her head. They all knew the place—an old estate along Morgantown Avenue, big and crumbling. The boys exchanged nervous glances. They'd never heard of Mrs. Mason having any children.

The car crawled forward. As they neared the estate, the girl stirred, suddenly alert. The vehicle stopped.

She thanked them in a hoarse whisper, opened the door, and ran toward the house. Disappeared inside.

One of the boys blinked.

"She's got my bandanna."

They decided to come back the next day.

**A Chill at the Door**

The following afternoon, they knocked.

Mrs. Mason, aged and slow, opened the door.

"Is your daughter home?" one of the boys asked.

The woman's face fell pale. Her mouth trembled.

"I... I have no daughter."

The boys explained. The girl in the snow. The blood. The ride. The bandanna.

Mrs. Mason shook. Her knuckles turned white on the edge of the door.

"My daughter died in a car accident years ago," she said. "She froze to death in a ditch. She never made it home." Her voice dropped to a whisper. "This is the fifth time someone's brought her back to me."

# The Headless Man of Graveyard Hollow

### A Ride into Terror

Long ago in Mobley, West Virginia, Roy Fisher and his neighbors, Zona and Opal Hibbs, were returning home from town with a wagon full of groceries. The night was bitter, the wind cruel, and the clouds hung low like they were waiting to fall. Halfway home, they began to climb a long hill, the horses' breath steaming like smoke in the cold air. At the top, they saw something.

A man.

A man without a head.

He stood in the road, waving a wide-brimmed hat in a slow, eerie circle like a lantern calling ships to wreck. The horses reared, their nostrils flaring, hooves pounding into the frozen dirt. They wouldn't move forward—snorting, whinnying, and stamping with wild terror.

The three riders sat frozen.

The thing did not.

It stepped forward.

## Through the Ghost

Roy gritted his teeth, grabbed the reins, and yanked them hard. He managed to wheel the horses back down the hill, then spun them again, driving them straight at the figure. The horses screamed—but they ran.

Straight through him.

The man's body flickered like smoke. He didn't move aside. He didn't resist. He simply passed through them.

And when they turned back, he was still there—waving his hat, walking calmly toward Graveyard Hollow. Then he vanished into the dark.

## Don't Follow the Dead

They did not follow. Everyone in Mobley knew better than that. You don't follow a ghost into a graveyard.

It's an invitation to misfortune—bad luck, worse fate, maybe even death. But more than that, it might not be just mischief. It might be a trap. Because sometimes, the dead come back for a reason.

And sometimes, they don't want to go back alone.

# The Witch and the Butter Churn

## Swarm on the Porch

A man lived with his wife at the edge of the woods, tucked deep where even the moonlight had to fight to find the ground. One late afternoon, as the wind whistled sharp through the trees, he set out on his porch to churn butter. He pumped the handle, slow at first, then faster. The thick, wet slap of cream echoed into the hollow. And then—he wasn't alone.

A cat appeared.

Then two.

Then six. Then twenty.

They crept from under the boards. Slunk from the trees. Dropped from the rafters. Black and gray, yellow-eyed and hissing.

They scratched at his boots. Bit at his legs. One climbed up his back, another onto his shoulders. Claws sliced through his sleeves and drew blood along his wrists. He swung at them and hollered, but they kept coming. Crawling over the churn. Tearing at his hair. A living, spitting blanket of fur and teeth trying to murder him.

### The Stranger's Knife

Out of nowhere, a stranger appeared at the edge of the clearing. Tall. Pale. Silent.

Without a word, he drew a knife from his belt and slashed through the mass of cats. One yowled—a high, ragged scream that didn't sound quite like an animal. As the knife came down again, there was a sickening *thock*.

A single paw, bloody and severed, fell to the porch floor. And then—nothing.

The cats were gone. All of them. Vanished into air like smoke blown by a sudden gust.

Only the paw remained, twitching. Still clawing at nothing.

### A Guest and a Groan

The man, shaken and bleeding, thanked the stranger and invited him in for a bite. They stepped into the dim, smoky cabin.

"Wife!" the man called. "We got a guest. Come meet him."

A low moan drifted from the back room.

"I'm too sick to get up," came a weak voice. "I can't make no food."

The two men stepped into the bedroom. There she lay—his wife—bundled to the chin in blankets, face pale as wax.

"At least shake the man's hand," the farmer said. "He saved my life."

She slowly raised her left hand.

"Your right hand," the man said. "Give him your right."

She didn't move.

Didn't blink.

Wouldn't speak.

The man's face darkened. His eyes narrowed.

In a flash, he grabbed the quilt and ripped it away.

There was no right hand.

Only a ragged, bleeding stump.

**Witch's End**

He said nothing.

Just threw the covers over her head.

Pressed them down.

And held them there.

The cabin was still for a long time after that.

And he never had trouble churning the butter again.

# Why They Avoid the Low Gap

### Where the Fog Hangs Heavy

In Wirt County, there is a place where the fog never lifts, where the air always tastes of iron, and something unseen walks between the trees. It's called the Low Gap—just below Belt Cemetery, tucked between two hills and always wet and always swampy.

They say the hauntings began with murder.

A merchant, a local businessman, was traveling home after dark. He never made it. Someone stepped from the shadows and fired a shotgun point-blank into his chest.

When he fell, twitching and gasping, the killer took a blade and sawed off his head. His blood soaked into the dirt road.

The thief tied the merchant's horses to a nearby tree. They stood there until morning, still as statues.

Since then, nothing good has come from that place.

## The Beast and the Fire

Travelers avoid the Low Gap. Those who don't often wish they had.

One man saw a great, dog-like creature lying in the road. It didn't flinch when he shouted. Didn't blink. He hurled a rock, and the thing lifted silently from the earth—hovered—and drifted over the hilltop into the trees.

It vanished.

Another night, two men walked through the gap, laughing at the old stories. Then a fireball—massive and hissing—came rolling down the trees. It didn't bounce. It didn't flicker. It pursued. They dove into the ditch, shaking. The ball hissed past and disappeared into the black.

They never laughed about ghosts again.

## The Jeweler's Dare

A local jeweler scoffed at the tales. To prove his point, he walked the Low Gap alone one night.

He came back pale and trembling. Wouldn't speak.

Then he blurted it out: he saw a man with no head. Standing in the darkest bend of the road. Then, it rose— floated—up toward the gap and drifted off into nothing.

He never set foot there again.

## The Lantern Man

One man, out late on foot, saw a lantern bobbing toward him. He called out. No answer. The figure grew closer.

And then—it was face-to-face.

And then—it was gone.

The man trembled. Stammered, "What's the matter? Did your light go out?"

A rough voice came from nowhere:

"No... my life went out."

A pale white form lifted from the road hovered in the air and sailed away toward the gap.

## The Long Way Around

No one goes that way now. Not if they can help it.

The Low Gap's quicker, sure.

But folks would rather add ten miles to their journey than risk catching sight of a lantern in the dark or hearing the soft hiss of something rolling through the trees.

Because sometimes, what's dead doesn't want to stay buried.

And sometimes, it wants to be seen.

Or to do bad things to others.

# Indrid Cold

### Encounter on the Highway

On the evening of November 2, 1966, as a bitter wind curled along the ridgelines and darkness swallowed the hills of West Virginia, sewing machine salesman Woodrow Derenberger was driving home from a business trip in Marietta, Ohio. It was nearing 7:30 p.m., and he was riding southbound on Interstate 77 near Parkersburg when he saw something that would haunt him forever.

A strange object—metallic, silent, charcoal-colored with a dull gray sheen—hovered above the pavement, blocking the highway. It floated just inches off the ground and looked like an enormous, squat kerosene lamp with a domed top and flat base. There were no lights. Just a soft, fluttering noise that brushed against the windows of his truck like a dying breath.

Then the thing opened.

A door cracked open like the door of a car, and a figure stepped out—a man or something wearing the skin of one.

## A Smile That Never Changed

The figure was between five and six feet tall, olive-skinned, with dark, slicked-back hair, and clothed in a shiny, glistening blue suit and trousers. His coat was short, and his shirt buttoned tightly to the top. He appeared to be in his late thirties or early forties. His expression never shifted. His lips didn't move. But he spoke.

"Have no fear," came the voice—not from his mouth, but from inside Derenberger's head. "We come from a country that is not nearly as powerful as yours. We mean you no harm."

The man smiled.

He never stopped smiling.

He introduced himself as Indrid Cold. His voice was calm, composed, terrifying in its pleasantness.

"Be not frightened." He said they ate. They slept. They bled, just like humans. But his eyes never blinked. His too-wide grin never faded.

Derenberger sat frozen in the cab of his truck, unable to speak, unable to scream.

The conversation lasted ten long minutes.

Then Cold turned. The door closed with a dull clunk.

And the craft lifted into the sky and was gone in an instant.

**The Others Who Saw**

Derenberger, trembling and pale, reported the incident to local police. But he was not alone.

Another man came forward—not long after—claiming a similar encounter. He, too, had seen the smiling man on Route 77, waving him down.

He did not stop.

The Lilly family of Point Pleasant began experiencing strange events around the same time. Their daughter, Linda, was found screaming in her bedroom one night.

She said a man had stood over her bed.

Grinning.

Too wide. Too still.

Eyes bright. Smile fixed.

They called him The Grinning Man.

They called him The Smiling Man.

But his name—if it was a name—was Indrid Cold.

And some say he's still out there.

Smiling.

# Thump-thump-thumpety-thump

**Where the Road Dies**

Big Run is an old road—part gravel, part dirt—that winds along the stream of the same name, fading into the hills and hollows like something trying to be forgotten. But it wasn't always like that. It used to stretch past Robey's farm, past the Sturm place, beyond old Elijah Freeland's hollow, past the one-room schoolhouse, all the way to Campbell Run Road.

Now it ends. There's a sign off US-250 that says so in big black letters: DEAD END.

But it doesn't tell you what kind of end.

## A Bitter Love and a Blood Debt

Years ago, that hollow held something worse than silence. Two young men—George Gump and Willie Jones—lived nearby. They worked the same soil, drank at the same taverns, and fought over the same woman: Helen Morgan.

She was beautiful, clever, and cruel in the way only someone adored by two rivals can be. One weekend, she'd ride with George to the picnic. The next, she'd sit beside Willie at the church sing. She kept them both close—and just out of reach.

Eventually, the game wore thin.

Willie made her choose.

She picked him.

They married. Six months later, Helen was with child. Willie was ecstatic. He hitched his buckboard and rode to town to buy her a bolt of calico fabric—a surprise for the future mother.

He stopped at the store. Then the bar.

It was nearly midnight when he headed home. His horse clopped along Big Run, the wheels of the buckboard thumping over ruts.

Willie smiled. One hand on the reins, one resting on the soft calico surprise beside him.

That's when someone climbed into the back of the wagon and changed everything.

## The Murder at Freeland's Hollow

It happened fast.

A blade flashed in the dark.

And in two brutal, wet strokes, Willie's head was severed from his shoulders.

A farmer nearby, driving hogs across the road, saw the wagon drift past on its own. Curious, he approached—and screamed. There, slumped over the spring-mounted seat, was Willie's headless body. His severed head rolled around in the back, thumping against the boards. *Thump-thump-thumpety-thump.*

The calico cloth flapped in the wind.

No one ever caught the killer.

But George Gump disappeared that same night.

He was never seen again.

## A Ghost That Rides

They say if you go to Freeland's Hollow at midnight when the moon is fat and full, you can still hear the sound of hooves. *Clippety-clop-Clippety-clop-clop-clop.*

A wagon creaking. *Creakety-creak-creak-creak.*

And in it—a headless figure clutching the reins, calico trailing like a bloody flag. *Flappety-flap-flap-flap.*

If you listen closely, you'll hear the *thump-thump-thumpety-thump* of something rolling loose in the back.

Something that was once a man's head.

So go ahead. Take the shortcut down Big Run.

Just don't say you weren't warned.

Because that road is a dead end in more ways than one—*thump-thump-thumpety-thump.*

# Flayed Ghost of Dorsey's Knob

**Blood on the Rocks**

In the mid-1700s, the land that would become Morgantown, West Virginia, was soaked in violence. Settlers pushed deeper into the wilderness, and Native Americans, their lands stolen and families slaughtered, fought back with all they had. One place, now known for its scenic overlook, was once a place of butchery: Dorsey's Knob.

To defend themselves, settlers built forts. One of these was Fort Cobun, a small stockade raised by the Jonathan Cobun family near the looming summit of Dorsey's Knob—a stony crown jutting over the Monongahela River. But no wall of timber could hold back vengeance forever.

In early spring of 1778, a group of settlers escorted by armed men were returning from planting corn. Hidden in the brush, Native warriors waited. The ambush was brutal. Shots rang out, screams tore through the air, and most of the party fled in terror.

But not all made it back.

### The Skinning of John Woodfin

Jacob Mill was shot through the belly. He stumbled, fell, and was hacked to death—tomahawked, then scalped where he lay.

But the fate of John Woodfin was worse.

Riding a horse, he made an easy target. A bullet shattered his thigh, and his horse crashed down upon him. Helpless, he was dragged away.

His captors took him to the top of Dorsey's Knob. In full view of the fort below, they planted two poles in an X shape and bound him to it. Then they peeled the scalp from his head and flayed him down the back of his neck.

They left him like that—bleeding, twitching, alive—until death finally found him.

Settlers watched, unable to help, as he bled out beneath the sky. His mutilated corpse remained on the hilltop for days, a gory warning to all who dared trespass.

## What Still Walks There

They buried what was left.

But something didn't stay down.

Now, those who hike Dorsey's Knob at night speak of a presence—a man in colonial garb, hunched and swaying, with blood-caked skin flapping from his neck like rotted ribbons.

His scalp is a glowing red veil, veined and dripping.

Sometimes, he's seen from the parking lot, standing still among the stones.

Blood dripping wet puddles.

Other times, hikers say he lunges from the dark, clawing for their heads.

They say he's searching—not for peace, but for skin.

Because when John Woodfin reaches out with bloody fingers, it's not to ask for help.

It's to tear a new face for his own.

# Greenbrier Ghost

## A Grave that Wouldn't Stay Silent

She rose from the earth with fury in her heart and a neck twisted beyond the grave—a ghost bent not on peace but justice. In 1897, Zona Heaster Shue clawed her way into West Virginia legend by pointing her cold, dead finger at her murderer from the other side. Zona lived in Livesay's Mill, a lonely mountain pocket in Greenbrier County. Her killer was her own husband, Edward "Trout" Shue, a handsome blacksmith who came to town with blue eyes, slick hair, and a past soaked in cruelty.

But it wasn't charm that followed Trout. It was blood.

## A Husband with a Trail of Corpses

He had already left scars behind. His first wife, Allie Cutlip, divorced him after he beat her half to death. Locals had even tossed him into the frozen Greenbrier River to punish him for his brutality. His second wife, Lucy Ann Tritt, married Trout at just sixteen. Less than eight months later, she was dead—rumor said he dropped a brick on her skull from a rooftop.

But nobody stopped him.

In October 1896, he married Zona.

## The Death of Zona

By January, she was dead.

Trout claimed it was childbirth. A doctor signed the death certificate. Zona was buried quickly—too quickly. But something wouldn't let her rest. Her mother, Mary Jane Heaster, began seeing visions. Zona stood at the foot of her bed, ghostly white, head lolling at an unnatural angle.

She told her mother the truth.

Trout had broken her neck.

## The Ghost Goes to Court

The body was exhumed. Zona's neck had indeed been snapped, her windpipe crushed, and bruises shaped like fingers wrapped around her throat.

The ghost had spoken true.

In court, Mary Jane Heaster testified to the visitations. The jury believed her. Trout was sentenced to life in Moundsville Penitentiary, where he later died.

## She Still Walks

Zona's ghost, they say, never left. Visitors to the tiny cemetery near the Soule United Methodist Church claim to see her drifting among the graves, veil flowing, head turned at an awful angle.

And if you hear your name whispered on the wind late at night near Meadow Bluff...

It just might be her.

Because Zona Heaster Shue doesn't forget.

And she doesn't forgive.

# The Feu Follet of Red Ash

## The Cry That Lures

Have you ever followed the sound of a baby crying into the woods?

The more you chase it, the farther it drifts—always just beyond reach. The trees twist around you. Time forgets its name. You stop knowing which way you came. Then, a flicker—a floating light, like a lightning bug or a lantern.

It pulls you forward.

Until you're lost.

## A French Spirit in West Virginia Soil

They call it the Feu Follet—a wandering spirit of a child who died before baptism, cursed to roam forever. It comes from old French folklore, but what's it doing here, in the misty swamp hollows of the New River Gorge?

French settlers, some descendants of Acadians, came to these lands before the French and Indian War. They brought their folklore with them.

## The Island of the Forgotten

There's an island near the ruins of Red Ash, a ghost town deep in the forest. The land is nearly lost to time. Years ago, it held pest houses—shacks for the sick during smallpox and Spanish flu epidemics. The dead were buried on the island, marked by crooked stones and rotting crosses.

They died in fevered sweats, writhing in agony. Some were miners blown apart in the black mouths of Red Ash and Rush Run. Others were babies.

Babies who wailed until their lungs tore.

Babies who died with no one to hold them.

Babies who never stopped crying.

## Into the Crying Dark

I was hiking the Southside Trail, following the New River past the coke ovens, when I heard it. A baby's cry, thin and desperate. I thought it might be a bird, some shrieking owl, or an odd migratory call. I followed it through the woods for nearly an hour.

Up one ridge. Down another.

The crying stayed ahead of me.

It wanted me to follow.

Eventually, orange flagging tape marked a trail. It led me to a graveyard—crumbling, sunken, quiet.

But the crying stopped.

Gone.

The wind stirred the canopy. Leaves crunched beneath me. Somewhere across the river, a train groaned on its rails.

But that baby was no bird.

It called out for warmth, for flesh.

It wanted me to find it.

**Don't Go Back**

They say the Feu Follet is lonely.

Hungry.

That it sometimes takes on a form that'll make you drop your guard—a crying child, a woman with her back turned, a flicker in the dark.

They say if it leads you far enough, you might forget you were ever real. Or you get lost.

And you'll stay with it.

Forever.

Somewhere, in the hollers by the river, beneath moss and grave dust.

Begging.

Crying.

Calling for someone new.

Not me, that time.

But later, maybe you—

# The Mumbler of Long Run

### The Tunnel That Time Left Behind

Far down the abandoned Parkersburg Branch—now part of West Virginia's Rails to Trails—past the Sherwood Tunnel and swallowed in thick forest, there lies a forgotten stretch of track and an old tunnel long since bypassed. It's overgrown. Rotting. Silent... mostly.

But not always.

### Voices from the Dark

It starts with a sound. Not a train. Not an echo. A mumble.

Low.

Uneasy. The words are never clear—just a voice drifting from the tunnel like breath from a corpse.

In 1927, a man heard it—talking in the dark. He followed it along the tracks. He followed it into the tunnel. He crept close and struck a match to peer into a manhole.

There was no one inside.

But the voice kept speaking. Mumbling. Grumbling. But about what, he did not know.

But the voice could only be connected to one thing—a murder so barbaric, it left a ghost.

### The Christmas Murder

Two nights before Christmas, 1924. 75-year-old James Powell—widower, farmer—was shot to death in cold blood at his homestead along the Parkersburg Branch of the B&O Railroad.

Three local boys robbed him. They took $65, a ring, and his watch. They missed a gold coin still tucked into his pocket.

The house was a bloodbath.

His family cleaned what they could, burying the blood-soaked clothing in haste on the property.

But winter rains unearthed the horror.

The bloody garments washed into the nearby pond.

And that's when the ghost began to rise.

### A Fire from the Pond

One night, Powell's son-in-law looked out toward the pond and screamed.

A face broke the water. His father-in-law's face.

Then—a blinding flare. A ball of fire exploded from the ghost's forehead like a Roman candle, searing through the night sky.

The family fled. No one lived there again. The house rotted into the ground.

The tunnel was forsaken and left to die.

But James Powell never left.

**He Still Walks**

Now, hikers hear the voice. Garbled. Rasping. Always just out of reach. They follow it along the old tracks. Some say they see the figure walking ahead—a shadow where there should be none.

He's wearing the same bloody shirt they buried.

They say if you listen closely, you might catch a word or two.

But those who get too close?

They say he stops talking.

And starts walking toward you.

Mouth still moving.

Eyes long gone.

And if you follow him in—if you let him lead you through the tunnel—

You'll never say a clear word again.

Just mumble.

And walk.

Forever.

But not alone. Oh no, never alone.

# The Shade of Shade Creek

**Back and Forth, Back and Forth...**

There's a creek near Victor, West Virginia, shrouded in shadow and sorrow, a place where the air grows cold even in summer.

They call it Shade Creek—not for the trees, but for what lingers there.

It's said a ghost walks that creek, trapped in endless grief, never to leave. It comes from an old tragedy, a tale the locals whisper but never tell too loud.

### The Blood Harvest

Long ago, a farm stood on a rise above the Midland Trail, the old buffalo road turned stagecoach line turned modern highway. One scorching summer day, a father swung his scythe in wide, monotonous arcs through a field of winter wheat.

*Back and forth, back and forth...*

The blade was curved and cruel, the cradle pressing the harvest against its brothers. The man worked in a daze, the kind born from sunstroke and repetition.

*Back and forth, back and forth...*

He didn't see his child slip away from the house.

Didn't hear the soft pat of tiny feet in tall grass.

Didn't know his three-year-old had wandered to the field, wanting to be near him.

*Back and forth*—THWACK.

The blade caught the child's throat.

Blood sprayed like rain from a storm cloud.

The father froze, the child spasmed, and the wheat drank deep of crimson.

He scooped the lifeless body into his arms and screamed all the way to the house. But there was no saving what was already gone.

### A Grave and a Curse

They buried the child beneath a tree by the creek. Then they left the farm, unable to stay. But something stayed behind.

Something that never stopped pacing.

Now, they say you can hear the scythe's whisper.

*Back and forth, back and forth...*

A shadowy figure moves through the trees, its head bowed, its hands dripping.

It mumbles in agony.

Some nights, a wail pierces the air so sharp it stops hearts in their chests.

*Back and forth, back and forth...*

The ghost of the grieving father is cursed to return.

*Back and forth, back and forth...*

To swing that blade.

*Back and forth, back and forth...*

To see that moment again and again.

*Back and forth, back and forth...*

And if you follow the sound to Shade Creek—if you're foolish enough to cross the bridge after midnight—you might see him.

And he might NOT see you.

And then the blade comes down.

*Back and forth, back and forth...*

*Back and forth*—THWACK.

# Old Rawhide of Riffle Run

## They Feared the Lonely and Isolated Stream

Riffle Run in Ritchie County is not far from the small town of Harrisville. It is a narrow, lonely stream that cuts through steep hollows and dense woods, the kind of place where fog hangs low and forgotten paths slip into nothing. Nowadays, the area is thick with undergrowth, broken stone fences, and the crumbled hints of old homesteads.

But long ago, it was feared—because something walked there.

## Old Rawhead

They called it Old Rawhead—a skinless, shambling corpse with a grin carved into bare bone. His name was once forgotten, but folks remembered his trade.

He was a tanner—one who worked hides, boiling and scraping the flesh from animal skins.

His cabin stank of blood, rot, and smoke.

But it wasn't the work that made people wary—it was the way he muttered to himself, the way the dogs refused to go near his land.

One autumn night, after weeks of storms and a blood-red moon rising through rain-slick clouds, the man began to scream. All night, the hills echoed with howls—not of pain, but rage.

By morning, he was gone.

Inside his cabin, they found horror: blood streaked the walls, buckets of skin sloshed beside his bed, and on the table, still steaming, lay his face.

Peeled clean.

His eyes gone.

His jaw was wide, and he was grinning.

A single bloody trail led from the cabin to the creek.

They say he walked into the water, still grinning.

Now, when the red moon rises, and the wind shifts in the hollows of Riffle Run, he comes back.

His bones clack like dice.

His skinless face shines wet in the dark.

He reeks of boiled flesh and tannery brine. Shreds of muscle drag behind him like butcher's rags.

He speaks only in rattles and moans. And he's always looking—for more.

One boy dared camp near Riffle Run and laughed off the stories. They found his boots the next morning—filled with blood and tucked neatly by the fire.

So, if you're walking near Riffle Run and you feel breath, you can't explain...

if the trees fall still...

if the fog thickens into something solid...

Don't run.

Don't scream.

Because Old Rawhead is watching.

And he's trying to remember how your skin would fit...on his face.

# Bloody Bogey

### The Bloody Bogey

Deep beneath the coal seams of McDowell County, where tunnels twist like intestines through the rock, there's a legend miners only speak of in whispers. They believe that if you say the name out loud, it opens a door—lets him through.

*Shhh.* It is called Bloody Bogey…

He's not a man. He was once. But now?

Now he's something worse. His flesh is gone, peeled back like wet paper.

His body is raw, red, twitching. The bones beneath glisten, slick and crimson, pulsing with a life that should have ended long ago. His grin never fades. He carries a jagged pickaxe that drips rust and ichor and rings out when no one's working.

*Tink-tink-tink.*

That's the sound it makes. It means he's coming.

Decades ago, a miner was crushed in a collapse—trapped, left to rot.

*Tink-tink-tink.*

He tried to break himself free. *Tink-tink-tink.*

But he couldn't.

They said he was dead. But they never found the body. Only blood. Smeared across the shaft like someone painted with it. And bones. Bloody bones. Laid out like they'd stood and walked away. Something took the rest. Something angry. Something hungry.

*Shhh.* Don't say his name. Bloody Bogey...

Miners working the graveyard shift tell of footsteps in shafts long sealed. Of lanterns dimming for no reason. Of steel dragging stone. Just before something grabs your ankle and pulls.

*Tink-tink-tink.*

*Shhh.* Don't say it. Don't look back.

But if you do... and if you do see Bloody Bogey—with his flayed grin and hollow sockets—pray your light holds. Because he hates the dark.

He wants your light.

And your skin. It is *soooo* warm and cozy.

# Evil Eye in Monongah

## A Town Shadowed by Coal and Curses

In the early 1900s, Monongah, a coal town in Marion County, bustled with immigrant workers from Hungary, Italy, and Poland. With them came the old-world fear of the Evil Eye—"boszorkány szem"—and stories that twisted like smoke through the hollers.

After the Monongah mining disaster of 1907 claimed hundreds of lives, grief lingered like a late fall mist. But darker whispers crept through the back alleys—tales of things worse than death.

One such whisper clung to a Hungarian widow who lived alone in a crooked white house at the edge of town. Garlic hung rotting above her door, and jars of fat and bones cluttered her shelves. She was said to talk to the crows, to weave rag dolls with twine and mutter into them.

Although most granny witches could be trusted, some could not. Those who crossed this particular granny witch's path said their cows soured, their infants wailed without cause, their teeth ached until they cracked. Her gaze, they said, could curdle blood in the vein.

### A Curse Through Hair

There was a girl named Lidia who fell ill—headaches that split her skull, fainting fits that left her limp and lifeless. Her mother, desperate, cut Lidia's long black hair to "lighten her head" and handed the braid to the old woman to burn, trusting the ancient ways.

But the woman vanished.

And Lidia worsened.

In a desperate search, Lidia's father stumbled upon a kettle buried deep behind the widow's house. Inside was Lidia's braid, steeped in vinegar and thorns, pierced through with a blackened iron nail.

A binding charm.

A tethering of soul to sickness.

He pulled it out with a stick—afraid to touch it—and burned it where he found it.

By sunrise, Lidia's headaches stopped. Her cries ceased. Her skin turned warm again.

### The Curse is Gone. But Where is the Granny Witch?

The old woman? She was never seen again.

But to this day, they say, if you walk Monongah's crooked streets and catch the scent of burnt hair on the wind—you best not meet the gaze of any stranger.

Because some eyes still curse.

Some witches never die.

And that particular granny witch is somewhere still around.

# Hellhound Under the Bed

In a coal town long buried by dust and soot, there lived a man known only for his cruelty. He was a mean old wretch who spat at children and cursed his neighbors from the front stoop of his sagging shack. No one liked him—and he liked it that way.

When typhoid fever took hold of his body, the town braced for a merciful silence. But pity outpaced hatred, and the same neighbors he scorned brought him broth, blankets, and care.

He cursed them as he always did.

Days passed, then weeks. On the final night of his life, a storm cracked the sky and lit his house in pulses of pale blue. He began to scream.

## The Black Dog Under the Bed

He wailed that a black dog was under his bed.

"Get it out!" he cried. "Get it out! It's growling and hot—burning me!"

They told him he was delirious, sweating through his fever, that there was no dog.

"I don't see it," he gasped. "I *feel* it. I know it's there."

A young man stooped to look. And there, beneath the bed, hidden in shadow, lay a monstrous hound—long as the bedframe, eyes like hot coals, steam rising from its ribs.

The smell of sulfur choked the room.

They tried coaxing it with meat. They tried poking it with a broom handle. But the beast would not stir. It simply watched the old man die with a slow, hissing breath.

Unable to bear the screaming, the neighbors fled the house.

## The Old Man Died

When they returned—the man was stone-cold dead.

And the hound was gone.

Some say it still appears when the wicked are dying, dragged by chains no one sees, sniffing out a soul that's bound for worse than worms. If you hear growling in the walls or feel a sudden heat beneath your bed—don't look. It's already seen you. Well, it has seen your soul.

# The Witch with One Glass Eye

Keeney's Knob rises like a crooked spine above the fog-choked forests of Summers County, its slopes forever cloaked in gloom.

It is a place where trees lean too close and paths twist where no paths should be.

### A Widow Lived on Keeney's Knob

High on that ridge lived a widow with a single glass eye. Sometimes she carried the glass eye in her palm, holding it before her like a charm, using it to see in the dark.

She was a woman shunned by locals who muttered darkly about her cursed marriage.

**She was Cursed**

Her husband had died deep in the mines after a cave-in, but before the rocks crushed him, he was heard screaming a curse on her name:

"You'll see what you did to me—even in the dark."

Not long after, the widow's home burned to the ground, leaving nothing but blackened stone and melted glass.

Yet her spirit was not at rest.

**Her Ghost Returns**

On moonless nights, when even the owls hold their tongues, a lantern can be seen bobbing in the woods around Keeney's Knob. Some say it's a trick of the mist.

Others know better.

If you are fool enough to follow it, you might glimpse her: a crooked figure stumbling through the trees, her tattered mourning dress snagging on thorns, her head cocked at a sickening angle.

One eye is dull and dead. But the other—the glass one—glows like a live coal in the darkness.

**And She'll Curse You, too!**

And if you get too close, they say she'll pluck your eyes out, laughing as she leaves you to stumble blindly through the woods...

# Rake Boy of Droop Mountain

## Blood in the Brush

In the waning months of the Civil War, Droop Mountain was a battleground soaked in blood. Union and Confederate troops camped there, thick with smoke, sweat, and starvation. In November of 1863, gunfire echoed through the trees—but one horror would not make it into any official report.

## The Boy and the Rake

Among the soldiers, a starving boy crept near a campfire, hoping to steal a hunk of bread or boiled meat.

But a soldier caught him. And instead of mercy, the man took up a grain rake—an iron-toothed monster of a tool—and beat the boy until his screams stopped.

They said the child's face was left in ribbons.

Torn.

Shredded.

Maskless.

**Buried in Rock and Silence**

They buried him quick, not deep. Just tucked under stones and brush as the army moved on.

No marker.

No prayer.

Only the flies buzzing.

**Crawling Through the Battlefield**

Now hikers say they see him.

Not standing—crawling.

A small figure moving low through the underbrush along the trails of Droop Mountain Battlefield.

His face looks torn by claws.

His eyes nothing but black pits.

**He Doesn't Speak**

He never says a word. He just drags himself through the leaves, and behind him, he leaves grooves in the dirt—deep, wide furrows like the tines of a rake.

And if you follow the trail long enough... it ends at your feet.

# The Bones and the Midwife of Mud Lick

## A Dangerous Line Between Healing and Damnation

In every remote Appalachian hollow, a midwife was as vital as a well or a woodpile. They came when the blood began to flow and stayed until a baby's first cry—or last breath. They knew herbs and prayers, but that knowledge walked a narrow road between medicine and witchcraft. And when the babies died, sometimes the whispers started.

## Miss Adeline's Garden

Miss Adeline was one such midwife. Thin as a rail, with a sharp tongue and eyes that never blinked, she lived alone on the edge of Mud Lick in a vine-choked shack. The women called her when labor came too early or too hard, and she'd arrive with a bundle of dried herbs and a pail of clean cloths.

But in 1913, a woman died giving birth—and the baby never breathed. When the townsfolk dug near Adeline's garden, they claimed to find strange, tiny bundles wrapped in linen under the squash vines.

Some say they were just dolls.

Others swear they were bones.

## Driven Out

The men came with lanterns and hickory clubs. They shouted "witch" and drove Miss Adeline into the woods with fire licking at her heels. No one knows where she died, but they say she cursed Mud Lick with her last breath.

## The Lullaby in the Fog

Now, when the wind comes off the creek and the night turns damp and cold, her lullabies drift through the trees—sung in a language no one alive understands. If the moon is low, you might catch a glimpse of her: a skeletal woman in a blood-stained shawl, gathering ghostly bundles in her arms and swaying as she sings.

## She Brings Gifts

Sometimes, after the song fades, a child's jawbone appears on a porch step. Wrapped in linen. Still warm.

# Black-beaked Watcher of Saltlick Pines

### A Thing Perched and Patient

In the crooked folds of Nicholas County, where pine needles crunch like dry bones and fog settles like breath on skin, farmers used to whisper of something that came when sickness spread—something in feathers.

They said it wasn't a man. Not anymore.

It wore a coat of black feathers slick with filth and soot.

Where a face should have been, it had a long, beak-like snout—stitched shut with rusted wire.

It never spoke. Never moved.

It perched on fenceposts. Barn roofs. Gate arches. Always crouched low, elbows resting on knees, its empty gaze fixed on something far worse than death.

**Omen of Blight**

Old-timers swore it came only during plagues or livestock sickness—like the hog cholera outbreak of 1929. When feed turned sour, and eyes festered white, that was when you'd see it. Waiting.

Watching.

A farmer near Saltlick spotted it squatting on his smokehouse roof and fired at it point-blank. The shot blew through—only feathers hit the dirt.

No blood. No meat.

Just a stench, like burned hair and rotting teeth.

**The Roosters Knew**

That night, every rooster on the farm screamed itself hoarse before dawn. The cows bellowed until their tongues hung limp. And in the morning, a bloody trail led from the hog pen straight into the woods.

They say the man moved away. He never told anyone what he saw when he followed the trail.

But the watchers in Saltlick Pines still swear: when you see it perched... don't look away.

If it knows you've seen it, it might open its beak.

And if the wire's ever gone—it means your name's already been called.

# The Wire Witch of Clover Lick

## A Lonely Hollow

Clover Lick in Pocahontas County was never much more than a stop along the Chesapeake and Ohio Railway, where the Greenbrier River carved its path and fog settled thick as wool.

In the early 1900s, scattered homesteads clung to the steep hills, and walking from one to the next took hours—sometimes days in winter. The isolation bred superstition, and from those shadows came her name.

### Cold as Wire

They whispered of a woman who lived alone near the creek bend. No one remembered her real name—only what they called her: *The Wire Witch*. She rarely came to town, but when she did, children fell sick soon after. Her fingers, it was said, were stiff and crooked, like rusty wire. Her touch was cold enough to burn.

One mother claimed her baby turned blue after the woman blessed it with a kiss.

Another swore her son's teeth turned black after the witch brushed his hair. No one could prove a thing.

### The Vanishing

In the winter of 1903, the woman vanished. Some said she froze in her cabin and was buried by the snow.

Others said she turned to crows and scattered to the trees. But long after, her curse remained.

### Trail of the Fingers

Today, hikers on the trail near Clover Lick swear they feel something brush the back of their necks—thin fingers dragging like wire across skin. If they stop, nothing's there. If they run, they trip. And sometimes, when the fog is thick, a shape appears on the trail just ahead: crooked, shrouded, bent in the spine.

### Coiled Warning

Sometimes, a length of coiled wire is found near where she walked, wrapped like a child's bracelet, still warm from a hand that is no longer flesh. And sometimes—just sometimes—if the wind is right, you'll hear a voice rasp from the trees: "Come. Let me make you cold, too."

# The Devil's Post at Rock Camp

### A Stone That Bleeds Lies

In the shadowed hollows of Monroe County, near the forgotten paths of Rock Camp, there exists a tiny rural crossroads settlement where an ancient fencepost stands unlike any other.

Weathered by time and elements, this jagged stone is said to possess a sinister ability to feel and comprehend. Locals whisper that it was once the site of a preacher's sudden death in 1889, a man who collapsed beside it under mysterious circumstances.

### The Cursed Marker

The post, often referred to as the Devil's Post, is reputed to react to deceit. It's said that if one places their hand upon it and utters a lie, the stone will grow warm, and blood will bead from the palm as if the rock itself weeps for the falsehood.

### An Omen of Misfortune

Over the years, tales have circulated of those who dared to challenge the post's power. One such story tells of a traveler who mocked the legend only to find himself plagued by nightmares and unexplained injuries.

Another speaks of a child who touched the stone and was later found speaking in tongues, eyes glazed with terror.

### A Warning to the Curious

Though the Devil's Post remains a physical landmark, many avoid it, fearing the consequences of its curse.

It's a relic of a time when the line between the natural and the supernatural was perilously thin.

It serves as a grim reminder: some stones are better left unturned.

# Granny Wiles and the Smoke-Sick Boys of Splinter Ridge

### The Witch of Splinter Ridge

They said she lived alone in a shanty stitched together, a gypsy-like wagon with rusted tin and handcart wood, hidden deep in the hemlocks past Splinter Ridge in Upshur County. Folks called her Granny Wiles, though she wasn't anyone's kin. She smoked a long pipe packed with God-knows-what and wore a necklace of dead baby birds, snake bones, and fangs from a raccoon.

Her eyes were yellow and slick, like chicken fat, and when she spoke, the wind stilled.

### Boys Who Coughed Black

One fall, two boys from the mining camp near Crow Hollow wandered up past her ridge. They said the mountains were changing color and wanted to hunt squirrels.

But when they came back down, they weren't the same.

Their skin had turned ashen, their eyes sunk deep into their skulls, and they coughed a thick, black smoke that stank like burnt hair and sour milk.

### "They Breathed Her Curse"

Old Doc Yeager said it was the consumption. But their mother swore otherwise. She said the boys had breathed in something awful from Granny Wiles' pipe smoke— that they'd wandered too close, that she'd blown her curse into their lungs.

Their cheeks turned pale, and their lips were rose-red.

Their bodies became gaunt and skeletal.

Then, the blood began to ooze deep red on the corners of their lips.

By winter, both boys were dead. They didn't just die.

They burned up from the inside, coughing smoke right to the end. Their lungs were found to be full of soot as if they'd been breathing coal fire.

### She Still Smokes

They burned her house down and ran her out. Or so they thought.

To this day, travelers on the old timber trail say they catch the scent of Granny Wiles' pipe—sweet and rotting. If you see a light flickering through the trees and hear the faint wheeze of breath and a cough like a smoker dying slowly, turn back.

Because she's still puffing that cursed pipe.

And she's always looking for more boys to smoke.

Or girls. Or anyone who gets in her way.

# The Knocking Woman of Stemple Ridge

### Preston County's Silent Harbinger
### Three Knocks at Dusk

In the 1920s, timber crews working along the cold ridgelines of Preston County spoke in hushed tones of a strange visitor. As dusk crept up the mountain, a woman in a black mourning dress would appear just outside their bunkhouses—never seen directly, only heard. Three sharp knocks on the cabin window.

Always three. Never more.

If a man was foolish enough to rise and open the door, he'd find nothing there—just the mist curling across the ground and a hush in the trees.

### The Death That Follows

By morning, someone in the crew would be gone. Sometimes, they found a body broken at the base of a cliff—snapped limbs bent backward, eyes wide with something seen too late.

Other times, nothing at all was found, just a trail of boot prints leading to the logging chute... and stopping at the edge.

They called her The Knocking Woman.

Not a ghost.

Not a witch.

Something older.

Something waiting.

### No One Knocks Back

Superstition soon spread:

*Never knock back.*

*Never answer.*

*Cover the windows with coats or coal sacks.*

*Hammer the doors shut after dusk.*

Men carved protective sigils into their bedposts.

Still, she came.

Some said she had no face—just a dark veil and pale hands. Others claimed her eyes glowed red in the blackness beyond the glass.

One man shot through the window after the third knock. He bled to death that night from an unseen wound across his back.

No one heard a gunshot.

Only the knocking.

**Where the Trees Still Listen**

To this day, hikers on Stemple Ridge report strange taps echoing in the brush. No birds. No wind. Just three slow knocks—one after another—coming from nowhere at all.

If you hear the knocks, don't turn around.

Don't speak.

And for the love of God, don't open a door.

# The Smiling Stranger of Pigeon Roost

### A Stranger Too Still Wearing a Dress Suit and Grin

Deep in the twisted hollows of Pigeon Roost in Logan County—where old mining roads buckle under moss, and the woods choke out the light—there were whispers of a thing that wore a man's skin but wasn't one.

He stood too tall, with shoulders sharp as sickles and a carefully pressed preacher's suit hanging off his bones like a death shroud.

He never moved but somehow always stayed ahead—no matter how fast you walked the winding paths.

His grin split his face in two, stretched ear to ear, wide and wet as if it had been carved there.

### The Thunderstorm Visitor

One summer night, as thunder rattled the rotted rafters and lightning clawed the sky, a woman in the hollow heard three sharp raps at her windowpane.

When she dared look out, there he was—his face nearly pressed against the glass, that endless, glistening and wet grin blooming against the storm. His knuckles were white and tight, his hands thin and veined like wax stretched too far.

The woman fainted cold. When she woke hours later, she found muddy boot prints smeared across her floor, leading from the window to the cradle where her dog once slept.

The dog was gone.

Only a pool of river mud remained.

### A Harbinger of Ruin

Some say the smiling thing was a harbinger—drawn by grief and sin, feeding on the rot that seeped up from the mines as the mountaintops were ripped apart.

Others swear it was something unearthed from deep in the black soil when man first started gnawing at the bones of the mountains.

Whatever it was, it still waits in the fog, standing too still, smiling too wide—waiting for the next soul foolish enough to meet its eyes.

# The Soot Widow

### Whispers in the Ashes

There was an old coal town. Born from the seams of black rock in the 1900s, fed on coal dust and fire. By the 1950s, it had swelled with over two thousand souls, a town stitched together by miner's grit and the ceaseless rumble underground.

But when the mines died, the heartbeat of the town slowed to a ghost's crawl. The shafts were sealed. The furnaces went cold. The dust settled—but not everything stayed buried.

They say when the last shaft closed, she began to walk.

A woman draped in a mourning veil so black it seemed to drink what little light the slag hills still caught.

Her skin was smeared with soot, her hands raw and cracked, her dress stiff with the ash of a hundred fires.

She moved along the slag heaps at dusk, dragging her fingers along the rusted grates of the sealed mine vents, whispering into the cracks like feeding kindling to old coals.

Old men—the ones who still smelled of cigar smoke and engine oil—said she had three sons.

Each of those boys were swallowed by the mines in different collapses, years apart.

They said when the last boy went under, she walked into the drift mouth after him.

She never walked out. Gone. But not—

**She Seeps Out of Old Mines still holding the Dead.**

Now, she returns to old coal mining towns that have gone to dust and mourns for all the boys who died within their dark depths.

She appears when the mist sags low, and the cinders crunch dry underfoot, her voice comes crawling up through the broken ground—thin and sharp, like a splinter sliding under the skin.

"Have you seen my boys?" she asks. "Have you seen my boys?"

And the ones foolish enough to answer — even in a whisper — don't stay themselves for long. Their eyes sink deep. Their mouths twist open in a shape they can't close.

Some say they're dragged down into the old seams, their nails scraping blood from the stone as they're pulled into the black.

So, don't answer. Walk away.

If you are taking old ghost town paths and see an old woman standing above an old mine shaft, walk on.

Don't look.

Don't listen.

And for the love of God, don't answer.

# The Ghosts of Monongah

### The Dead That Couldn't Leave

In the cold December of 1907, the mines beneath Monongah, West Virginia, heaved once — and swallowed the town whole.

An explosion deep underground tore through Fairmont Coal Company Mines No. 6 and No. 8, snuffing out 362 men in less than an hour — the deadliest mining disaster in American history.

Fathers, sons, brothers — whole bloodlines broken and blackened in a single breath.

The bodies they could reach were charred to ash or broken into pieces too small to carry out.

But many were never recovered at all.

The tunnels were sealed. The air was left to rot.

The living fled Monongah in droves.

But not everything stayed buried.

**Whispers in the Drift**

Old miners, the ones too stubborn or too poor to leave, spoke of strange things in the years that followed.

They said that sometimes, when the wind slipped down the slag heaps and into the hollow shafts, you could hear knocking — rhythmic, desperate, echoing up from the sealed mines.

Not the creaks of settling earth.

Not the groan of old timbers.

Knocking, like fists beating against a coffin lid.

At night, ghost-lights — dim, flickering orbs the color of bone and smoke — floated over the slag heaps. Some swore they saw the shadows of miners still trudging across the yards, faces hidden behind soot-smeared handkerchiefs, lamps swinging low. In town, a few claimed to hear voices rising from storm drains and cellar grates — broken voices calling for water, for light, for air. "We're still here," they whispered. "Still here. Still burning."

And more than one poor soul who answered — who dared to peer down into a vent or shaft mouth — was said to fall sick within days, their lungs filling with black dust, their skin turning pale as the dead.

## If You Hear the Knocking

The old-timers had a rule, passed down through the last families that stayed:

If you hear the knocking, don't knock back.

If you see the lights, don't follow.

And if the voices call your name—*run.*

Because not every grave holds quiet bones.

And not every ghost means you well.

# The Headless Horror of Logan County

### The Hollow That Swallowed Him

*"No head, no breath, no soul to save—*

*Stay out the drift, or you'll dig your own grave."*

In Logan County, the coal ran deep and numerous — and so did the graves of those who worked in the mines to extract it.

The mines there were treacherous, cutting through the mountains like a labyrinth of rotten veins.

Men went in every day with their lamps trembling on their caps and their lungs filling with dust thick enough to chew.

One winter morning, after a shaft collapse, they dragged out the bodies.

All but one.

When they found him, he was still standing—half-pinned under a splintered beam.

His hands were clenched so tight around his pick that it took two men to pry it free.

And his head was gone.

Crushed? Blown clean off? Nobody agreed.

All they knew was that something was missing, and the ground where his head should've lain was blacker and wetter than the rest.

The foreman ordered the shaft sealed.

Better to leave whatever still crawled under there in the dark.

### The Thing That Walked Out

The first sightings came within the month.

Men working late claimed they saw a figure stalking the haul roads — shoulders slumped, bloody collar gaping open where a head ought to be.

Some said it carried a pickaxe still dripping black mud.

Others said it just wandered, arms dangling loose, dragging its fingers along the walls with a sound like meat slapping stone. At night, if you listened close, you could hear it—a wet, shuffling noise, and something hollow, like breath scraping through a broken flute.

One miner who stayed too late swore he glimpsed it at the edge of his lantern light. The headless miner was sitting where the mouth of the mine used to be.

By the time the others found him, he'd almost clawed his own eyes out, trying not to see.

They said he died babbling about "the thing that forgot it was dead."

### If You Hear the Pickaxe

Old-timers in Logan County still warn:

If you hear a pick tapping slow on stone—don't look behind you.

If your lamp flickers and the walls seem to breathe — run.

And if the tunnel ahead goes too quiet, and the air starts to taste like old blood—get out.

Because the Headless Miner is still searching.

For his way out.

For his head.

Or maybe just for someone else's.

# The Headless Woman of Briar Hollow

### Where the Briars Took Root

Briar Hollow was the kind of place you didn't enter unless you had no other choice.

A crooked pocket of Greenbrier County, not far from Rainelle — a place smothered in thorn and rot, where the woods tangled so tight you could barely tell day from night.

It wasn't always that way.

They say once there was a house there — a miserable lean-to of a farmstead, its walls sagging and its fields stubborn with stone.

But in the late 1800s, something wicked soaked into the dirt. The man who lived there—bitter and brutal even by mountain standards—caught his wife in a jealous rage.

Maybe it was a look, maybe it was nothing at all.

Either way, by the time the sun fell, her body lay twisted in the yard, her throat hacked so deep her head hung by a strip of flesh.

He vanished into the forest, and the hollow devoured what was left.

The house buckled, the fenceposts sank, and the briars — thick, black-thorned, and hungry — crept over everything like fingers closing into a fist.

Some said the land itself had taken sides.

Some said it just liked blood.

## The Hollow's Mourner

Not long after the killing, travelers passing through Briar Hollow at night began to talk.

They spoke of a woman in a torn white dress, staggering blindly through the thickets, her arms locked around the ragged stump of her own neck.

Her head was gone. Just a stub, dark and glistening in the lantern light, as she groped at the empty air where her face should have been. Dogs refused to go down the path — they would drop their bellies to the ground and howl until their throats gave out.

Even the bravest hounds bolted, tails between their legs, at the scent of the hollow.

Lanterns—strong, well-trimmed—would shudder and snuff as you neared the treeline.

Some said it was the weight of the hollow itself, pressing the life out of the flame.

Others heard her before they saw her.

Low sobbing, broken gasps threading through the briars, always just beyond the reach of the light.

A sound like someone trying to cry without lungs.

Those foolish enough to chase the voice — to push through the thorns after the sound — didn't always come back.

And when they did, they came back torn, bloodied, whispering about a white dress flashing through the trees, about hands that reached up from the earth and pulled.

### The Curse in the Vines

The old folks around Rainelle would warn you plainly:

On nights when the fog hugs low, and the wind knots in the trees, the briars in that hollow are not just plants.

They grab.

They bite.

It wasn't just scratches that the wanderers came back with — it was gouges, ripped sleeves, skin peeled raw like something trying to drag them down into the roots.

And if you left a patch of your blood behind?

They said it gave her just enough to follow you home.

Some ghosts are tied to the ground.

Some, to the sin that soaked it.

And in Briar Hollow, the ground remembers. And so do the local children who once chanted this rhyme:

"Where the briars grab,

the dead still roam —

lose your way, and

she'll drag you home."

# The Ghost of Harpers Ferry Train Tunnel

## Where the River Cut Through Bone

Near Harpers Ferry, where the mountains sag heavy against the sky and the Potomac gnaws the stone raw, the railroad carved its black veins deep into the heart of the earth.

The Big Tunnel was a wound from the start — a moist, gasping hole torn through the ribs of the mountain.

Men died digging it.

Blown apart into wet scraps of meat.

Crushed flat under slabs of weeping slate.

Drowned, gasping mud and river water, when the rock gave way without warning.

But it wasn't the dying that made men fear the Big Tunnel.

It was what they saw after.

### The Lantern Swinger

The tracklayers, the wall-bracers, the hard men with soot ground into their bones — they began to talk, low and bitter when the whiskey ran out.

Of the thing that waited where the darkness of the tunnel began.

Not flesh.

Not shadow.

Something caught between.

He wore the battered rags of a miner—heavy leather boots eaten by rot, a soot-black shirt torn along the seams, a slouch cap jammed low over a caved-in ruin of a face.

One arm dangled at a crooked angle, the lantern at its end swinging wild and broken.

And his mouth—his mouth gaped and worked, over and over, trying to scream, to warn—but no sound ever came.

He never crossed into the daylight.

He stood right where the blackness swallowed the stone — just beyond reach, just behind the breath of the mountain.

Always at dusk or just after the last engine light had faded and the damp rose from the river like cold fingers.

When the tunnel exhaled, it stunk of old iron, dead water, and rotted breath.

The men who saw him tried not to speak of it.

But those who did—their eyes constantly shifted to the floor, their fingers picking at the frayed edges of their sleeves—said the ghost would raise a ruined hand, swinging that battered lantern like a noose.

And if you dared step closer, the light would die—and the figure would vanish into the black.

And then the mountain would take its payment.

A roof caving in with a scream like tearing skin.

A coupling chain snapping loose and shearing a brakeman in half.

A man slipping silent from the ledge and disappearing into the hungry river without a splash.

The Big Tunnel wasn't just cursed by the blood spilled to birth it. It was kept alive by what it refused to spit out.

**The Warning They Left**

Old hands at Harpers Ferry would mutter warnings to green boys:

If you see a swinging light where no man should be, don't follow it. If you see a man trying to shout but hear no sound, turn back. If the tunnel exhales colder than the night air, walk fast, and don't look behind you.

Because the ghost in the Big Tunnel wasn't trying to scare you.

He is trying to tell you — you are next.

# Creepy Things Our Old Folks Used to Do

**(Most *not* recommended. Ask a doctor first)**

## Signs of Death and Misfortune

### Dog Howling at Midnight:

→ A dog howling at the stroke of midnight foretells a death before the next new moon.

### Bird Flying into the House:

→ If a bird comes inside the house, death is near.

### Bread Won't Rise:

→ Bread dough that refuses to rise means a corpse is lying nearby.

### First Rain after Burial:

→ Rain soon after a burial means the soul was accepted into heaven.

### Sweeping After Sundown:

→ Sweeping dirt out the front door after dark sweeps away your luck and invites sorrow.


## Love Signs and Marriage Foretellings

### Full Moon Well Reflection:

→ Look into a well under a full moon — you'll see the face of the one you'll marry.

### Counting Stars Nine Nights:

→ Count nine stars nine nights running, and on the ninth night, your true love will appear in your dreams.

# Old Folk Cures

**Curing a Cold:**

→ Wear an asafetida bag on the neck to prevent a cold.

**Curing Warts with Bacon:**

→ Rub a wart with raw bacon, bury it under a rock by the waning moon — as the bacon rots, so will the wart.

**Coffin Nail Toothache Cure:**

→ Hammer a nail into an oak tree while whispering "take it from me"—tree will take your toothache away.

**Stopping Nosebleeds with Red String:**

→ Tie a red string tight around your left ring finger to stop a nosebleed.

**Hair Cutting by the Moon:**

→ Cut your hair during a waxing moon for thick growth; cut during a waning moon if you want thin hair.

# Warding Off Evil and Bad Spirits

**Throwing Salt Over Your Shoulder:**

→ If you spill salt, toss a pinch over your left shoulder to blind the Devil waiting behind you.

**Whistling Indoors:**

→ Never whistle inside the house — it calls spirits that don't belong.

**Carrying a Graveyard Rabbit's Foot:**

→ A left hind foot of a rabbit caught at midnight in a graveyard wards off witches and bad luck.

# Ways to Get Bad Luck:

→ It is bad luck to leave the house by a door different from the one you entered.

→ Never lay your hat on the bed, it is bad luck.

→ To avoid bad luck, always put on the left shoe first.

# Deeper Mountain Signs, Cures, and Warnings
## Death, Curses, and Bad Luck Signs

**The Screaming Dog**:

→ If a dog screams like a woman at night, it means death is already in the hollow.

**Sow Eats Her Litter**:

→ If a sow eats her piglets, the farm is cursed.

⇢ Cure: Bury a live chicken under the threshold of the barn to lift the curse.

**Moth at the Door**:

→ A white moth banging at your door means a ghost is seeking entry.

**Sparrow Flying Under the Eaves**:

→ A sparrow nesting under the eaves brings a death within the year.

# Strange Folk Cures

**To Cure Cradle Death (Sudden Infant Death)**:

→ Slip a sharp knife under the baby's mattress to cut the "witch's thread" tied around the child's soul.

**Witch Blood Cure**:

→ Stab a witch's footprint in the mud with a rusty nail; it will make her sicken and break her hex.

**Swallowed Spider Cure**:

→ Swallow a live spider wrapped in butter to cure an inflamed throat. (Horrifying, so don't)

# Weather and Protection Signs

**Snake Skin to Stop Lightning:**

→ Nail a dried snake skin to the barn beam to keep lightning from striking the building.

**Bury a Jar of Nails:**

→ Bury an open jar of old nails under the hearth to protect the house from witchcraft and fire.

**Plant an Onion by the Door:**

→ An onion planted at the front steps keeps sickness and witches out of the home.

# Signs from the Grave

**Deathwatch Beetle:**

→ If you hear tapping in the walls at night — three slow knocks — it's the Deathwatch Beetle. Someone in the house will soon die.

**Corpse Light on the Hill:**

→ If you see a blue flame flickering over a graveyard or a hill, a fresh grave will be opened within days.

**Grave that Sinks Too Fast:**

→ If a grave sinks within three days of burial, the spirit is restless and may walk.

# Citations

•westvirginiamountainmama.com/2016/11/01/hallowee n-visit-to-the-haunted-lunatic-asylum

• flickr.com/photos/itinerant wanderer/5140457659

• Weston State Hospital / Trans-Allegheny Lunatic Asylum Construction & Operations

• West Virginia Division of Culture and History Archives

• National Register of Historic Places (1978)

• "Asylum: Inside the Weston State Hospital" by Mark Davis

• West Virginia Archives and History: Civil War Records Collection

• Library of Congress Civil War Cartography Collection

• West Virginia Folklore Collection (WVARHC)

• The quote in your story ("There is an old man who walks with a lantern...") comes from these collections (Field Note 1938-C.D.-WVARHC-07).

• Trans-Allegheny Lunatic Asylum Official Tour Materials & Guide Interviews

• Reported first-hand by multiple tour guides; local oral tradition supports the claim of a woman named Ruth with violent behaviors.

• "Haunted History: Trans-Allegheny Lunatic Asylum" (TV special, Travel Channel, 2011)

• Ghost Adventures: Season 4, Episode 2 – Trans-Allegheny Lunatic Asylum (2010)

• Dark Tourism West Virginia: Firsthand Accounts of the Asylum, by Patrick Hite

• WV Paranormal Investigators Field Reports, 2008–2016

• Tourist testimonies archived in Trans-Allegheny Lunatic Asylum guest books (physical onsite, also partially quoted in

Davis' Asylum).

• Trans-Allegheny Asylum Tour Narratives (special "VIP" tour records from 2000s onward)

• Interviews with restoration staff found in local newspaper: Weston Democrat, 1995–1996

• Wvhistoryonview.org/

• WPA Folklore & Field Notes Collection (Library of Congress):

    • loc.gov/collections/federal-writers-project/

• Staunton-Parkersburg Turnpike Alliance oral accounts.

• "West Virginia Ghost Stories and Legends" by folklorists like Ruth Ann Musick.

• Taylor County historical society notes and Civil War troop movement records.

• Local legends cited in newspaper clippings and anecdotal interviews from Wood County records.

• tumblr.com/haunts-of-the-world/62006886652/west-virginia-turnpike

• Donnelly, Shirley. "Ghost Stories from Local Towns." Beckley Post-Herald (April 1965). [West Virginia Ghosts] Beckley Post-Herald & The Raleigh Register Beckley, West Virginia Sat, Apr 17, 1965 Page 4

• elkinsrandolphwv.com/place/staunton-parkersburg-turnpike

• trans-alleghenylunaticasylum.com/

• wvghosts.com/true-stories/other-encounters/the-legend-of-the-screaming-thing/

• Witchcraft and the Devil in West Virginia RUTH ANN MUSICK Appalachian Journal, Vol. 1, No. 4 (Spring 1974), pp. 271-276 (6 pages)

• Musick, R. A. (1965). The telltale lilac Bush: And other

West Virginia ghost tales. University Press of Kentucky. A Head and a Body

• Hoosier folklore bulletin. (1949). FOLKLORE FROM WEST VIRGINIA By Ruth Ann M

• West Virginia Ghost Stories Ruth Ann Musick Midwest Folklore, Vol. 8, No. 1 (Spring, 1958), pp. 21-28 (8 pages) THE GIRL WHO HAD BEEN IN AN ACCIDENT (Contributed by Doris Summers, former student at FSC.)

• Witchcraft Magic and Spirits on the Border of Pennsylvania and West Virginia S. P. Bayard The Journal of American Folklore, Vol. 51, No. 199 (Jan. - Mar., 1938), pp. 47-59 (13 pages)

• WPA Writers' Project Notes (1930s) — collected local ghost and workman's tales, including mentions of spectral figures at Harpers Ferry tunnels.

• B&O Railroad oral histories — brakemen and tracklayers passed along ghost sightings through late 1800s–early 1900s.

• Local newspapers occasionally mentioned ghost stories from Harpers Ferry and Sandy Hook in late 19th-century "curiosity" articles.

• MUSICK, RUTH ANN. "Witchcraft and the Devil in West Virginia." Appalachian Journal, vol. 1, no. 4, 1974, pp. 271–76. JSTOR, jstor.org/stable/40931993. Accessed 25 Apr. 2025. Contributed by Mrs. Bertha Tichenor of Fairmont, about 1950

• Indrid Cold: The Raleigh Register Beckley, West Virginia Fri, Nov 4, 1966 Page 1

• Musick, R. A. (1952). Omens and Tokens of West Virginia. Midwest Folklore, 2(4), 263-267.

• The Devil's Post of Rock Camp is derived from Monroe County, West Virginia oral folklore, preserved through regional ghost story collections, WPA 1930s folklore projects, and privately recorded family legends.

• Patrick Gainer (West Virginia Folklore) and regional WPA ghost accounts

• Oral histories of Pocahontas County, WV; folklore patterns documented in the WPA Federal Writers' Project Folklore Collections (1930s); local Droop Mountain Battlefield ghost stories.

• Negro Tales from West Virginia John Harrington Cox The Journal of American Folklore Vol. 47, No. 186 (Oct. - Dec., 1934), pp. 341-357 (17 pages) Contributed by Mr. W. E. Chilton, Jr., Charleston, Kanawha County, April 16, 1925

www.ingramcontent.com/pod-product-compliance
Lightning Source LLC
Chambersburg PA
CBHW070020260626
47159CB00005B/1886